The Wedding Date

By Cara Connelly

The Wedding Date

Coming Soon
The Wedding Favor

The Wedding Date

A CHRISTMAS NOVELLA

CARA CONNELLY

AVONIMPULSE

An Imprint of HarperCollinsPublishers

Excerpt from *The Wedding Favor* copyright © 2013 by Lisa Connelly.

Excerpt from *The Wedding Vow* copyright © 2014 by Lisa Connelly.

Excerpt from *Rescued by a Stranger* copyright © 2013 by Lizbeth Selvig.

Excerpt from *Chasing Morgan* copyright © 2013 by Jennifer Ryan.

Excerpt from *Throwing Heat* copyright © 2013 by Candice Wakoff.

Excerpt from *Private Research* copyright © 2013 by Sabrina Darby.

EPub Edition December 2013 ISBN: 9780062282231

Print Edition ISBN: 9780062282248

10 9 8 7 6 5 4 3

For Mom. She'd be so proud.

Chapter One

"BLIND DATES ARE for losers." Julie Marone pinched the phone with her shoulder and used both hands to scrape the papers on her desk into a tidy pile. "You really think I'm a loser?"

"Not a *loser*, exactly." Amelia's inflection kept her options open.

Julie snorted a laugh. "Gee, thanks, sis. Tell me how you *really* feel."

"You know what I mean. You've been out of circulation for three years. You have to start *somewhere*."

"Sure, but did it have to be at the bottom of the barrel?"

"Peter's a nice guy!" Amelia protested.

"Absolutely," Julie said agreeably. "So devoted to dear old Mom that he *still lives in her basement*."

Amelia let out a here-we-go-again groan. "He's an optometrist, for crying out loud. I assumed he'd have his own place."

Julie started on the old saying about what happens when you *assume*, but Amelia cut her off. "Yeah, yeah. Ass. You. Me. Got it. Anyway, Leo"—tonight's date—"is a definite step up. I checked with his sister"—Amelia's hairstylist—"and she said he's got a house in Natick. His practice is thriving."

"So why's he going on a blind date?"

"His divorce just came through."

Julie groaned. Recently divorced men fell into two categories. "Shopping for a replacement or still simmering with resentment?"

"Come on, Jules, give him a chance."

Julie sighed. Slid the stack of papers into a folder marked "Westin/Anderson" and added it to her briefcase for tomorrow's closing. "Just tell me where to meet him."

"On Hanover Street at seven. He made reservations at a place on Prince."

"Well, in that case." Dinner in Boston's North End almost made it worthwhile. Julie was always up for good Italian. "How will I recognize him? Tall, dark, and handsome?" A girl could hope.

"Dark . . . but . . . not tall. Wearing a red scarf."

"Handsome?"

Amelia cleared her throat. "I caught one of his commercials the other night. He's got a nice smile."

"Whoa, wait. Commercials? What kind of lawyer is he?"

"Personal injury." Amelia dropped it like a turd. Then said, "Oh, look, Ray's here. Gotta go," and hung up.

Putting two and two together, Julie groaned. Leo

could only be the ubiquitous Leo "I Feel Your" Payne, whose commercials saturated late-night television, promising Boston's sleepless that he *would not quit* until they got every penny they deserved—minus his third, of course.

"How did I get into this?" she murmured.

For three years, since David died, she'd tried explaining to her sister that her career, her rigorous training schedule—she really *would* do the marathon this year—and their sprawling Italian American family kept her too busy for a man. And Amelia, even though she didn't buy it, had respected Julie's wishes.

Until now.

The catalyst, Julie knew, was Amelia's own upcoming Christmas Eve wedding. She wanted Julie—her maid of honor—to bring a date. A real date, not her gay friend Dan. Amelia loved Dan like a brother, but he was single too, always up for hanging out, and he made it too easy for Julie to duck the dating game.

So Amelia had lined up three eligible men and informed Julie that if she didn't give them a chance, then their mother—a confirmed cougar with not-great taste in men—would bring a wedding date for her.

Recognizing a train wreck when she saw one coming, Julie had given in and agreed to date all three. So far they were shaping up even worse than expected.

Jan appeared in the doorway. "J-Julie?" Her usually pale cheeks were pink. Her tiny bosom heaved. "Oh Julie. You'll never believe . . . the most . . . I mean . . ."

"Take a breath, Jan." Julie did that thing where she

pointed two fingers at Jan's eyes, then back at her own. "Focus."

Jan sucked air through her nose, let it out with a wheeze. "Okay, we just had a walk-in. From Austin." She wheezed again. "He's *gorgeous*. And that drawl . . ." Wheeze.

Julie nodded encouragingly. It never helped to rush Jan.

"He said . . ." Jan fanned herself, for real. She was actually perspiring. "He said someone in the ER told him about you."

That sounded ominous.

Julie glanced at her watch. —5:45. Too late to deal with mysterious strangers. If she left now, she'd just have time to get home and change into something more casual for her date.

"Ask him to come back tomorrow," she said. "I don't have time—"

"He just wants a minute." Jan wiped her palms on her grey pleated skirt. At twenty-five, she dressed like Julie's Gram, but inside she was stuck at sixteen, helpless in the face of a handsome man. "I-I'm sorry. I couldn't say no."

Julie blew out a sigh, wondered—again—why she'd hired her silly cousin in the first place. Because family was family, that's why.

"Fine. Send him in."

Ten seconds later, six foot two of Texan filled her door. Tawny hair, caramel eyes, tanned cheekbones.

Whoa.

Her own sixteen-year-old heart went pitty pat.

He crossed the room, swallowed up her hand in his

big palm, and said in a ridiculous drawl, "Cody Brown. I appreciate you seeing me, Miz Marone."

"Call me Julie," she managed to reply. Her hand felt naked when he released it, like she'd pulled off a warm glove on a cold winter day.

No wonder Jan had gone to pieces. He was tall, the way an oak tree's tall. Lean, the way a cougar's lean.

She gestured and he took a seat, his beat-up leather jacket falling open over an indigo shirt with pearl snaps and a belt buckle the size of Texas. When he crossed one cowboy-booted ankle over the other snug-jeaned knee, spurs jangled in her head.

Her mouth went dry.

She picked up her pen, clicked it off and on, off and on. "So, you're new to Boston?"

Cody Brown unfurled a slow, eye-crinkling smile. "What gave me away?"

She huffed out a laugh. "Okay, that was dumb."

God, she was as bad as Jan.

He waved a hand. "Not at all," he drawled, "you were just being polite." The December wind had stirred up his hair. The fingers he raked through it did nothing to tame it. "You're right, I'm brand new to Boston. Just got here last week, and been working every day since I touched down."

"I see," she said, staring at his stubble, the way it shadowed his jaw. She made herself look down at the yellow pad on her desk. "Are you looking for a house? A condo?"

"I'm thinking condo."

She made a note. "Your wife agrees?"

"I'm not married."

She glanced up. "Engaged?"

He shook his head. "No girlfriend either. Or boyfriend, for that matter." He broke into that smile again.

She set her pen on the desk. "Who referred you to me?"

"Marianne Wells. Said you found her dream house."

Julie remembered her, a nurse at Mass General. "Yes, I found a house for her. For her and her *husband*." She put an apology in her smile. "That's what I do. I match couples with houses."

Cody tilted his head. "Just couples? How come?"

"It's my specialty."

He nodded agreeably. "Okay. But how come?"

She shifted impatiently. "Because it is." *And that's all the explanation you're getting.* "Now, Mr. Brown—"

"It's Cody to my friends." He smiled. "Most of my enemies too."

She wished he'd holster that smile. It lit up the room, exposing how drab her office was. Tasteful, of course—ecru walls, framed prints, gold upholstery. But bland. She hadn't noticed just how bland until he'd walked in and started smiling all over it.

She clicked her pen.

His smile widened and a dimple appeared, for God's sake.

Then he spread his hands. His big, warm hands. "Julie," he said in that slow, Texas drawl. "Can't you make an exception for me?"

She tried to say *no*, to resist his pull. But he held her

gaze, tugging her irresistibly toward blue skies and sunshine.

Her breath gave a hitch, her stomach a dip.

And her heart, her frozen heart, thumped *at last*.

CODY'D THOUGHT HE was too damn tired for sex, but from his first glimpse of Julie Marone—moss-green eyes, chestnut hair, slim runner's body—he'd been picturing her out of that business suit and spread across his bed, wearing a lacy pushup bra and not another damn thing.

Then her breath caught, a sexy little hiccup, and he was halfway hard before he knew what hit him.

Damn it. He didn't need to get laid half as much as he needed a place to live. After seven straight overnights in the Mass General ER—and an eighth that would begin in just a few hours—he was finally due to get some time off. Four days, to be exact, which gave him exactly that long to find a condo, sign the papers, and write the damn check.

But Julie wasn't cooperating. Not only did she have his cock in an uproar, she wasn't inclined to hunt up a condo for him. She kept feeding him a line about *couples*, like she was some kind of karmic matchmaker or something.

Seriously, what kind of Realtor gave a shit who she sold to? A house was a house; a condo was a condo. Money was money. Right?

Whatever. She was hot for him too, and even if he wasn't in a position to do anything about it right at the moment, he wasn't above using it to get what he wanted.

Deliberately, in a move that had yet to fail him, he put his palm to his chest, rubbed it back and forth slowly.

Her eyes dropped to follow the movement.

He let her think about it.

She swallowed.

Then, shamelessly, he worked his drawl. "I'd sure be grateful if you'd help me out. I been staying next door at the Plaza—and don't get me wrong, it's swanky, for sure—but I need my own place so I can bring Betsy on east with me."

Her eyes snapped up. "I thought you didn't have a girlfriend."

"Betsy's my dog. Part coonhound, part Chihuahua." He did the smile again. "She'll like you. You both got that feisty thing going on."

Her brow knitted, and he bit his cheek to hold back a laugh. She probably wasn't sure how to feel about being compared to his dog. He could tell her it was a compliment—Betsy was the only woman who'd never disappointed him—but he didn't want her to get cocky.

What he wanted was for her to forget her cockamamie rule about couples and find him a condo in the next four days. That meant keeping her interested in him. So he played his strongest card, the one that worked with all the ladies. Worked too well in fact. But he wasn't going to argue with that now.

"The problem's my schedule," he went on, spreading his palms. "Me being a doctor and all."

He waited for her to rip her clothes off.

She didn't.

For five long seconds, she stared straight into his eyes. Then she opened a drawer and took out a business card, set it on the desk in front of him.

He dropped his eyes. *Brian Murphy—Century 21.*

What the fuck?

"Murph's a friend of mine," she said, her voice cool and flat. "I'm sure he can help you." She snapped her briefcase shut.

Cody couldn't believe it. The doctor thing *always* made women go crazy. So crazy that they stopped seeing Cody Brown the man and saw only Cody Brown, MD, their ticket to a McMansion in the burbs and vacations in Cabo.

But this chick was the opposite of attracted. She'd gone downright frosty.

He was in uncharted territory.

Desperate, he went into full seduction mode, hit her with the eye-lock, sexy-smile combo, playing it out in super slow-mo.

First he caught her eyes. Held them. Let a long, silent moment slide by like a river of molasses.

Then slowly, leisurely, as if he had all night to get it done, he curved his lips. First one side. Then the other.

She paused.

He deepened his drawl. "I want *you*, Julie."

She clicked her pen.

"Give me one day," he crooned. "Just tomorrow, that's all."

Click click. "Are you sure you wouldn't rather rent first? Check out the neighborhoods?"

He shook his head. "I'm not picky. Someplace close to Mass General will do me fine, where I can take Betsy for a run."

She hesitated, obviously wrestling with some inner demon.

He put his money on the horny Realtor.

"Beacon Hill could work," she said at last.

Not a smidgen of smugness seeped into his voice. "That where the Old North Church is? One if by land, two if by sea?"

She smiled, finally, a pretty sight. "No, that's in the North End. You could look there too, especially if you're a fan of Italian food. The restaurants are amazing."

He stood up. So did she. She was taller than he expected, which meant she had long legs.

He liked long legs.

"Let's go try one out," he said like it was only natural. "I'm sick of room service."

She looked startled. "Oh. Um. Thanks, but I have a date." She gave a nervous laugh. "A blind date, actually. And a closing in the morning."

"Seriously?" he blurted.

Her eyebrows shot up.

He did damage control. "A closing in the morning? I shouldn't be surprised. You must have lots of those." He nodded, sagely. Wondered why in the hell a looker like her had a *blind date*.

One of her brows came down, but she arched the other like she was assessing his intellect, wondering if he was actually smart enough to be a doctor. Then she lifted her briefcase and came around the desk, herding him through the door. "I can give you tomorrow afternoon. I'll line up a few places, and we'll get started around one."

"Sure. Let me give you my number." Maybe she'd get lonely, give him a booty call.

"Give it to Jan," she said, sticking a fork in his fantasy.

In the outer office, Jan looked like a Munchkin behind her oversized desk. "Take Dr. Brown's number," said Julie, on a march to the door. "Then go home. I'll check in after the closing." And she was gone.

"Well hell," Cody muttered. She'd blown him off. What about the eye-lock, sexy-smile combo? He was *sure* that'd put her in heat.

Huh.

He turned to Jan. A new sparkle lit her eyes.

"You're a *doctor*?" she said.

He let out a sigh.

Chapter Two

JULIE SHOULD HAVE been feeling the warm glow of a job well done. The million-dollar fixer-upper in Newton, Boston's priciest suburb, was the Andersons' dream house. And she'd made it happen for them.

That was what she did, matched happy couples with the homes of their dreams. It wasn't just her livelihood, it was her calling. It kept her busy, fulfilled. And ever since David died and she'd had to let go of their dream house, it had kept her sane.

But at the moment, the warm glow she was feeling had nothing to do with tomorrow's Westin/Anderson closing, and everything to do with Cody Brown.

In fact, it was more of a slow burn than a warm glow. Julie scowled at her subway-window reflection. In under twenty minutes Dr. Sex-Me-Up had exploded three of her hard-and-fast rules: Couples only, dream houses only, and no doctors in her life in any way, shape, or form.

To top it off, thanks to him she'd run out of time to go home and change clothes. She'd have to sit through dinner with Leo Payne in a perfectly tailored suit that she knew from experience would shrink two sizes at the first bite of pasta.

Damn Cody Brown and his stupid dimple.

Still grinding that axe as she trudged down Hanover Street, she blamed Cody for her three-inch ankle breakers as well. Then she spotted a red scarf at the corner of Hanover and Prince. And instantly regretted her heels all the more.

Amelia had warned her that Leo wasn't tall. But she hadn't mentioned that he was actually *short*. Julie would have an inch on him barefoot. In her heels, she towered over him.

Leo, at least, didn't seem to mind. He gave her an appreciative once-over. "Hi, Julie. It's great to meet you."

"You too," she said. He seemed genuinely nice. She made up her mind to give him a chance.

Then he went up on his toes to buss her cheek, and her determination flagged.

Shallow, she told herself. *Shallow, superficial, primitive female, secretly hungering for a caveman.*

Not coincidentally, an image of Cody flashed through her mind. She shut it down hard. Let Leo take her arm as they crossed Prince Street.

He ushered her into the dimly lit foyer of a slightly upscale but otherwise typical North End restaurant, the kind of place where she was used to getting a great meal served by heavily accented waiters who knew how to wink at a woman without her date catching on.

Leo stage-whispered to her, "I get treated good here. The maître d' had a slip and fall at the Stop & Shop. A runaway cherry tomato." He arched a meaningful brow. "They're the most dangerous vegetable, you know."

She grinned, grateful that he had a sense of humor . . . until his serious expression told her he wasn't joking.

Oh boy.

Leo's erstwhile client showed them to a cozy booth, all red leather and candlelight. Sinatra crooned in the background. As they slid into their seats, Julie made herself ignore Leo's pudge—anyone would look pudgy compared to Cody—and fanned the embers of optimism, struggling to keep it alive.

But as the waiter uncorked an expensive red and Leo started to download, the last spark fizzled out.

First he took her through the divorce, subtitled "Who Cheated on Who First." Then the property distribution, down to the last Enya CD. And finally the custody battle, best described as bludgeoning each other with the children.

Then the salads arrived.

It was too cliché to be true. But when nobody sprang out to shout "Candid Camera," Julie dug in with a fervor, willing her entrée to follow apace. Why, oh why, had she ordered the wild mushroom risotto when the menu specifically warned that it was made to order?

Wine helped. So did bread, warm and slathered with butter. She hit it hard, felt her waistband tighten. Promised herself she'd run it off in the morning.

Her thoughts strayed to the marathon. For three

years, she'd thought about running it but never seemed to have the time—or, let's face it, the discipline—to train. This year, she'd printed a training schedule off the Web, and with four months to go she was on track and feeling physically better than she had since David's death.

Leo touched her arm. She did a mental head shake. "Sorry. Did you ask me something?"

"I was saying that I get carried away when I get going on my ex."

Ah, a glimmer of self-awareness. Julie cut him some slack. "It's obviously still raw."

"I guess it is." He smiled, ruefully, and Julie softened some more. He had a nice smile. Strong jaw, white teeth, full lips.

She smiled back.

"So you've never been married?" he asked.

"I was engaged, but my fiancé passed away."

"I'm sorry," he said, and the sincerity in his voice went a little further toward rehabilitating him. "Was it an accident?"

"An illness. He had brain cancer."

"That sounds awful." He touched her arm again, a comforting pat that actually had that effect on her.

It occurred to her that he probably had lots of practice comforting trauma victims as he solicited their business, but she dismissed that thought as uncharitable even for her. "Yes, it was awful. Cancer's awful."

"I lost my mom to cancer." He sketched an air circle in his chest area.

She cut him more slack. He wasn't really *that* short.

The risotto arrived, and it was creamy deliciousness. Leo ordered another bottle of wine, turned the topic to Christmas shopping, and they spent some time bemoaning the traffic at the malls, then moved on to the Pats and their chances of making the Super Bowl.

And then, just as Julie was starting to relax, a stray leaf of lettuce slithered off a passing tray.

Onto the Tuscan tile it plopped, an oily menace three steps from their table. Instantly alert to the personal injury potential, Leo gasped and rose to avert disaster.

Too late. A middle-aged woman in heels higher than Julie's stepped on it and sailed through the air. It happened in a blink; her feet left the ground, her arms flew to the sides. She landed on her ass, taking out a waiter with a tray full of pasta, who sideswiped a busboy and his pan of dirty dishes.

Crockery shattered stupendously, silencing the place. For five seconds, at least, nobody moved.

Nobody except Leo, her hero, who was already in motion. He reached the woman first, untangling her from the heap, swiping spaghetti from her cheek. Asking if she'd hit her head, hurt her back, bruised her hip.

Too dazed to answer, she watched dumbly as he whipped out his phone and hit 911.

Then others mobilized. A patron helped the waiter to his feet. The maître d' helped the busboy, then handed him a mop.

Only the woman remained on the floor, guarded by Leo, attentive and in charge. Julie could only admire his Good Samaritan spirit.

Until, that is, the EMTs came in and crowded him out. Then, as he gave the woman's hand a last encouraging squeeze, he slipped a business card into her palm.

CODY TAPPED A finger on the bar, and the pretty bartender set another cold one in front of him. Sam Adams, Boston's finest.

Ignoring the glass, he tipped the bottle, glanced up at the game. The Celtics, what else? Boston fans were rabid. Red Sox, Bruins. The Patriots, for Christ's sake.

He could get on board with the beer, but the Pats? Forget about it.

His veggie burger appeared, half buried under fries. He poked it with his finger. Overdone, of course. No surprise. He'd long ago accepted that bar menus weren't designed with vegetarians in mind. He drowned it in ketchup and hot sauce. He could eat an old boot like that.

Taylor Swift whispered through the sound system. A couple canoodling over their wine kept drawing his eye. He had to laugh at himself. For his first thirty-three years, he wouldn't have given them a glance. Now envy gnawed him. Hit-and-run relationships had lost their thrill. He wanted what those two had—eyes only for each other.

For a couple of months there, he thought he might have found that with Bethany. But all it took was proposing to her to find out she was as bad as the rest of them, just looking for a doctor who could give her a country club lifestyle.

Hell, maybe he should've stayed on the family ranch

with his brother Tyrell. That way, if a woman came after him, he'd know she was interested in him, not just his earning potential. The irony was, Ty made shitloads more money running the ranch than Cody'd ever make as a doctor. But women didn't get it, and he was sick of fighting the stereotype. For now, he'd rather be lonely—and damn it, he *was* lonely—than give his heart to another social-climbing beauty queen, no matter how nice her rack.

He was getting set to head back to the Plaza for a pre-shift nap when the blonde who'd been eyeing him from the end of the bar broke away from her gaggle of girlfriends and shimmied her fine ass onto the stool beside him.

"Hey, cowboy." Her smile was friendly. "What brings you to Beantown?"

He looked down at himself, then back at her. "Is it the boots?"

"Nope," she said. "I couldn't even see them from where I was standing." She cocked her head, assessing. "I think it's the vibe. You're too laid back for Boston."

"Folks do seem in a helluva hurry here." He signaled the bartender to bring her the drink Texas courtesy required.

She smiled her thanks, then flipped her hair over one slender shoulder. "You've got all of us speculating. The smart money's on undercover federal marshal hunting down a fugitive"—she waggled her fingers to show that was her bet—"but there's also a vote for billionaire oilman slash venture capitalist, and one holdout for ex-ballplayer turned scout."

"And you got elected to unlock my secrets?"

"Not exactly." Her hazel eyes twinkled. "We sort of auctioned you off, and I won."

That pulled a laugh out of him. "Well, honey, I hate to disappoint you, but I'm just a doctor."

Her shoulders slumped. Her eyes fell. "Is that all? Just a doctor?"

For a moment he thought she really was disappointed, and his spirits rose. Julie Marone hadn't been impressed either. Maybe Boston women were different. Maybe doctors weren't considered a catch in this town.

Then the blonde lifted her head and there it was, the avaricious gleam in her eye. His own shoulders drooped. He could really like this girl. She was smart and pretty and funny, and he could use a friend in this town.

Now all he wanted was to get away from her.

Peeling a few bills from the roll in his pocket, he dropped them on the bar and stood up. The girl's eyes widened. "Wait. You're leaving? You didn't say what kind of medicine you practice. Or where you live. Or if you've got a girlfriend."

"I'm an ER doc," he said, "which means shitty hours and not-great money. I live in a hotel. And my girl Betsy's moving in with me next week."

She deflated. "Oh. Well, it was nice meeting you." She rallied with a smile, and Cody felt a twinge of regret for another relationship that died before it was born.

Lifting a hand to the gaggle, he walked out the door and into the lonely night.

Chapter Three

THE CLOSING WENT off beautifully. When the empty-nest
Westins turned the key over to the newly pregnant Andersons, Julie felt more than just the satisfaction of a job
well done; she felt joy, made all the brighter and deeper by
the wistfulness that limned it.

Back at the office, she handed off the fifty-thousand-
dollar commission check to Jan. "You can bring that to
the bank and take the rest of the day off."

It was their routine after closing a big sale, and Jan
was obviously expecting it. Her huge purse squatted on
her desk, ready to go. "I'm getting a mani/pedi," she said.
"Wish you could come with me."

"So do I." Feeling resentful, Julie held out her hand for
the pink slip with Cody Brown's number on it. "I can't
believe I let him rope me into this."

"I can." Jan giggled. "I'd let him rope me into just about
anything. Then he could use that rope to tie me up—"

"Jan Marone!" Julie was shocked. "I told you not to read *Fifty Shades*!"

"And it was the worst advice you ever gave me." Jan dug through her purse, past the kitchen sink, and came out with a dog-eared copy of the first volume. Tugging the pink slip from Julie's fingers, she stuck it in the middle of the book and handed it to Julie. "See you Monday. Meanwhile, have fun with Dr. Do-Me."

Slack-jawed, Julie watched her formerly repressed cousin scoot out of the office. Then she shook the pink slip out of the book. She certainly would *not* have fun with *Dr.* Do-Me.

Maybe if he'd been plain old Cody Brown, she would've considered it, because even she had to admit that three years without sex was two years, eleven months, three weeks, and six days too long. But losing David had shriveled her libido along with her heart, and even though both had finally stirred to life when Cody walked into her office, she wasn't going there with a *doctor*. Not a chance.

She'd learned all she needed to know about doctors when David was ill, starting with the neurologist who wrote off his headaches as migraines—until the MRI they insisted on revealed the tumor. After that, he'd shuffled them off to a surgeon, who'd pushed them on to an oncologist, who passed them off to a radiologist . . . In all, David had seen a dozen doctors, and each one—each almighty specialist—had offered them hope but brought only misery. Surgery. Radiation. Chemotherapy. All had hurt David, and hurt Julie too, because watching him suffer was a brand of torture all its own.

And when their miracles inevitably failed, each one of those high-dollar doctors wrote it off to statistical probabilities and pushed David down the line without a backward thought. Until finally, there weren't any more specialists, and he was left to walk the last leg of his journey alone, with only Julie and the wonderful hospice nurses at his side.

Oh yes, she'd had enough of doctors to last a lifetime.

So why, why, why had she taken Cody on? What was she thinking?

She *wasn't* thinking, that was the problem. She was feeling. And those feelings were all wrong. They'd suckered her into this BAD IDEA. And if she wasn't careful, she'd make a BAD MOVE. Which, with a *doctor*—who was a player to boot—would certainly lead to a really BAD ENDING.

She could only hope he was as motivated as he claimed. With luck, he'd jump at the first place she showed him, and she'd be rid of him before she made another mistake.

She dialed his number, got his voicemail: "It's Cody. Start talking." She hung up. Damn him. She didn't want to drag this out.

Outside, a sleety December drizzle came down from a leaden sky. Cars *shissed* past, spraying sludge. She sprinted next door to the Plaza and marched straight up to the desk. "I'm looking for Dr. Brown," she informed the pretty brunette with the "Ashley" nametag. "Can you ring his room?"

Ashley broke into a smile. "Oh, Cody's not in his room. He went down the street to Starbucks." Looking up over Julie's shoulder, her smile widened. "Here he comes now. And he's got my latte. Isn't he sweet?" She sighed.

Julie turned around. And sure enough, here came Cody, swaggering across the ultra-opulent lobby, a dozen gilt-framed mirrors ricocheting his reflection off every wall. Even if she'd tried, she couldn't escape the golden streaks in his hair, or the stubbly, sun-kissed jaw. She couldn't ignore the nut-hugger jeans that served up his package on a plate, or the battered leather jacket, unzipped to display a rain-spattered T-shirt plastered to his paving-stone abs.

Ashley sighed again.

Julie set her teeth. Okay, so he didn't look like any doctor she'd ever encountered. So what?

Then he ran a hand through his dripping hair, pushing it back from his brow, and her mind's eye blinked like the shutter on a camera. As clear as a bell, she saw him saunter from her bathroom, towel slung around his hips, wicked smile on his lips, shoving back his wet hair as his honey brown eyes walked the length of her very naked body.

The image was so real, so breathtakingly vivid, that her hand flew to her cheek; she could've sworn she felt beard burn.

He pulled up beside her, smiled down into her eyes. "If I knew you'd be here, I'd have brought you a latte."

His drawl was a feather that whispered over her skin.

Then Ashley butted in. "Cody, the hospital called. They said you weren't answering your cell."

It hit Julie like a slap, snapping her out of her spell. The hospital, that's where he belonged, not barging into her bedroom or her visions.

Taking a *looong* step back in both body and mind, she headed for the door. "I'll wait outside," she threw over her shoulder.

"It's raining," Cody called after her, but she kept moving, out onto the sidewalk.

Pausing under the awning, she unbuttoned her coat, flapping it open and closed. She was too young for hot flashes. This heat was all Cody.

For three years she'd been frozen up like a glacier. Why was she melting down now, at the wrong time, with the wrong man?

He was a doctor, damn it! He belonged in a white coat, in a dreary office, spewing nonsense to hapless patients who didn't know better than to trust him. But instead her traitorous body—not to mention her stupid psychic eye—had him stripped down to his birthday suit, waltzing across her bedroom like he owned the place.

No way could she spend the afternoon with him. She'd have to tell him that something came up, she couldn't help him after all.

But she couldn't tell him to his face. Oh, no. He'd smile all over her and she'd knuckle under again.

She'd call him, that's what she'd do. Then there'd be no crinkly eyes, no dimple. No stupid sexy stubble. On the phone she could behave like the mature professional she was.

With a last fleeting glance, she turned her back on the door—and ran.

STEPPING OUTSIDE, CODY glimpsed Julie's red coat disappearing around the corner. What the hell? He couldn't have been more than two minutes, and she'd ditched him.

Before he could ask himself why he didn't just let her go, he took off after her.

She moved fast, but Cody was faster. He might walk like a snail, but he ran like a jaguar, even in cowboy boots. He spotted her going down into the T and he poured on the gas, caught up to her before she shot through the turnstile.

When he touched her arm, she jumped a foot. "What the hell?"

"That's what I'd like to know," he said. "I turned around and you were gone."

Her cheeks were flushed. "I-I thought the hospital needed you. That you'd have to go."

"It's my first day off in a week," he said. "It'd take a plane crash to get me back there today."

"Don't you have patients? Don't you think they might need you?"

She sounded pissed, though he couldn't see why. "I'm an ER doc. I treat traumas. Accidents, gunshots, food poisoning."

That seemed to befuddle her. "So you don't have your own patients?"

"No, I treat 'em and pass 'em on."

She stiffened again. "So you just shunt them through the system? You don't take responsibility for them, or follow up to see whether they live or die?"

"I keep 'em alive, Julie. That's my job. Then I move them along to docs who can treat them long term." He plowed a hand through his dripping hair, spattering raindrops. "Can we get out of this weather? Find someplace warm and talk about what's bothering you?"

"Nothing's bothering me."

Yeah, right.

"Then let's find someplace warm and get lunch." He tried the smile, though he was starting to doubt its mojo. She seemed semi-immune to him. One minute she looked like she wanted to eat him up, the next she was trying to dish him off on some other Realtor, or running away from him altogether.

He had to admit she'd caught his interest, but was she really worth all this trouble?

Then she opened her coat, flapped it a few times, and he got an eyeful. Her white silk blouse was wet, glued to her bra and transparent as glass.

He jerked his eyes up to her face before she noticed him staring, but the lacy pattern was burned into his retinas.

He redoubled his efforts.

"Julie, honey," he drawled, "I been up all night. I've got to eat or hit the sheets, one or the other." A raindrop rolled down her cheek. He thumbed it off, couldn't resist adding, "You're welcome to join me for either."

She rolled her eyes. "Does that line really work?"

"You tell me."

She flapped her coat again.

He kept his eyes on hers. Rubbed his jaw so the stubble rasped.

She looked away. Fought the demon again. Finally threw up her hands. "There's a pub around the corner. But no dawdling. I'm giving up my afternoon off for this."

"Now I feel guilty," he said as they trotted up the steps to the sidewalk. He pulled off his jacket, held it over their heads. Rain streamed off the edges, washed down their backs. At least Julie had her coat. He was immediately soaked to the skin. "Let's call it off. Head up to my room for a hot shower."

She snorted. "I thought you were sick of the hotel and desperate to find a condo? Poor Betsy in the kennel and all that."

"Betsy's living large at my brother's ranch," he said, tucking her against his side. "And I'm thinking I can put up with the hotel a little longer."

Hell, if it got Julie out of her wet clothes, he'd put up with it a *lot* longer. He'd plant a fucking flag and call it Texas.

Chapter Four

JULIE HAD BEEN propositioned before. It wasn't all that unusual.

What was unusual was her overheated reaction to Cody's invitation.

She'd kept a grip on herself enough to compromise with lunch instead of bed, but as she looped an arm around his waist for the sprint to the pub, she wondered if there was such a thing as compromise with Cody, or if he was an all-or-nothing kind of guy.

They ducked inside, two drowned rats dripping on the floor. The hostess station was deserted. Julie hung Cody's jacket and her own drenched coat on hooks. Turned around in time to see him wring out his T-shirt, then flap it a few times. She got a glimpse of his abs, and goose bumps rippled up her arms. She told herself she was chilly.

Then he shook his head like a dog, spattering water off his hair.

She leapt back. "Hey!"

He laughed. Came closer. Opened his arms.

She backed up a step. "Don't even think about it."

"Oh, I'm thinking."

"I'm serious, Cody."

"Me too, Julie." He grinned an evil grin that raised goose bumps again. "I'm gonna get you wet."

She caught his double meaning. "Don't," she said, but her voice snagged on the word.

He took another step. His eyes had gone hot. "Beg me," he said, his voice gruff now, and deep.

Another step. She couldn't move, couldn't speak. Her heaving breasts bumped his chest.

"Beg me," he whispered, locked on her eyes.

Her tongue touched her lips. They were dry.

She was wet.

Slowly, he lowered his lips to her ear. "Julie," his warm breath fanned her skin, "I'm counting to three. One." He licked a raindrop from the lobe of her ear. "Two." He bit down, tugging ever so lightly. "Three." His arms came around her, crushing her to his sopping chest.

It should have felt awful. Cold and slimy. Instead it felt hot and sweaty and totally awesome. His chest was a wall, his arms iron bands.

And his crotch, well that was just ridiculous. She hadn't pressed against a hard-on in way too long, but she remembered how it felt, and this was in its own class.

"Cody," she got out, a feeble protest that sounded more like a give-it-to-me moan.

"Julie," he growled, buried in her hair. "You smell so fucking good. I could eat you up."

It hit her veins like straight whiskey. She wriggled and squirmed, not fighting him, but trying to get closer. Every cell, every sinew, even her bones and her breath, all of her strained toward him, begging him, begging him.

He answered with a moan, cupped her ass in his hand. She rose up on her toes, raked her nails down his back.

Then a throat cleared loudly. "Would you like lunch?" an amused female voice asked. "Or would you rather get a room?"

Shocked back to her senses, Julie shoved against Cody's chest. He let her go in his own sweet time. Asked her the same question with his eyes.

"Lunch," she answered both of them. She smoothed her skirt. "By the fire, if it's going."

In the cozy bar, the hostess waved a hand toward a loveseat by the hearth. In the brick fireplace, flames crackled invitingly. "Silent Night" played through the speakers over the bar, the Irish Rovers giving it a Celtic twist. The red-haired waitress swung by, and Julie asked for hot tea and a scone. Cody ordered two grilled cheese sandwiches, a double salad, and banana cream pie.

"And bring me a hot coffee with that," he added, smiling all over the poor girl. When she tottered away glassy-eyed, Julie made a face.

"What?" Cody said. "What'd I do?"

"Oh please. Like you don't know."

"Seriously, enlighten me."

"You smiled at her."

"Well hell, lock me up."

"You should be locked up. Better still, you should have to go through one day without being able to smile, just to see how the rest of the world lives."

"Admit it, honey. You'd miss it more than I would."

She rolled her eyes, then made a point of ignoring him as she unzipped her leaky boots, went to toast her butt by the fire.

He came up beside her, held his hands out to the flames. He was even taller now that she was flat-footed. She fought the urge to look up at him, but she could feel his smile heating up the whole left side of her body.

"You can forget it," she said. "I'm not gonna look."

His laugh rumbled up from his incredible chest. "You sure it's the smile? Maybe you're just into me."

She sniffed, derisively. "I'm not *into* you. You *jumped* me."

"Well, what do you expect, showing off your bra like that?"

She gasped and looked down. Slapped a hand to her chest. "Why didn't you tell me?" She slewed a glance around the bar. Nobody was looking, but she felt half-naked.

"It's all right," Cody said. "I wouldn't let anybody else ogle you."

"But it's okay for *you* to ogle me?"

He shrugged. "Figured you were trying to seduce me. A man can hope."

Now why did that make the blood rush in her veins?

The waitress showed up with their drinks. Cody made a point of smiling at her. Julie ignored him.

Back on the loveseat, she stirred sugar into her tea, kept one hand on her chest. Fought the urge to lean into his big warm body. Why was she so attracted to him when all she wanted was to hate him?

Oblivious to her inner battle, he gazed into the flames, sipping his coffee, his palms curled around the oversized mug. She shifted in her seat, remembering those big palms squeezing her ass, tugging her up against his—

"Seems funny," he said out of the blue, "the couples thing. How'd you decide on that?"

She dragged her mind out of the gutter, did a casual shrug. "It's a marketing thing."

He caught her eye. "Bullshit."

That surprised her. "Why would I make it up?"

"I don't know. Why would you?"

She wasn't going there, not with him.

She let her gaze stray to the mantle, decked with pine boughs and red felt stockings, names written in glitter on the snowy white trim.

She used to love Christmas and all of its trappings. But that was something else that died with David—her Christmas spirit. Now the holidays reminded her of hospitals. Hospitals and doctors. And death.

"Why'd you decide to be a doctor?" She couldn't keep the tension from her voice. Doctors should be objects of contempt, not lust.

"Not for the money, if that's what you're thinking."

"God complex?" She'd met more than a few who thought they were omnipotent.

"I wanted to save lives," he said without getting defensive. "Never saw myself in the ER, though. Always figured I was more cut out for research than blood and guts."

She rolled her shoulders, dialed back her resentment to a manageable level. Tried to remember that he wasn't one of the white coats who'd made David's last months hell.

"Okay. Then how'd you end up in the ER?"

"Just about the time I was deciding on my residency, a drunk driver wiped out my brother's wife. The ER docs kept her alive, but in the end, she didn't make it." He rolled his cup between his palms. "After that, it seemed like the way to go. Maybe save somebody else's wife. Or kid."

This conversation wasn't going where it was supposed to go. She should be hating him, not hating *herself* for *not* hating him.

She didn't trust her voice, so she kept still. Made a project out of her first sip of tea.

After a few moments of silence, he circled back to his original question. "So how come you only work with couples?"

She hesitated. Why not tell him? He'd shared something of himself with her. And it wasn't like she'd see him again after today. Jan had been angling to do a closing. She could handle his.

"I've got a knack for it," she said, "matching couples with their dream houses. Basically, they tell me what they're looking for, what's important to them, and I can just . . . see the house."

She raised a hand, palm out, expecting derision. "I know it sounds hokey. Believe me, I don't tell many people that it's like a psychic thing. Next thing you know they'd want me to find their lost cat. But there it is."

She waited for the smirk. Even David had teased her. Gently, because he didn't know any other way. But his doubts were apparent, and she'd often wished she hadn't told him.

But Cody didn't laugh. His sandwiches arrived. He ate the first one in four bites. Then he wiped his lips with his napkin and turned his warm eyes on hers.

"My Gramps was Apache," he said. "A shaman."

"Is that a psychic?"

"More like a mystic. He believed in a spirit world. Said he had visions of things before they happened." Cody shrugged. "Why not dream houses?"

"So . . . you're not freaked out? Most people look at me like I have two heads. They think I'm either lying or scary."

"I'm not scared." He chomped a fry. "And as far as I can tell, the only lie you told me was to deny your gift."

She sat back. Studied him. Was he pulling her leg? Suckering her into more embarrassing revelations?

"So the house you closed on today," he said, "that was a dream house?" He seemed genuinely curious.

She decided to trust him. "A 1920s colonial, partially restored. Brick fireplace in the living room. Sugar maples out front, overgrown grape arbor in back."

Cody eyed her. "Must feel good."

"Terrific. They'll be cutting their first Christmas tree by now, deciding which window to put it in." She tried to keep the wistfulness from her voice.

"Ever have visions about other things?"

Cody-in-a-towel popped into her head. "Um, not reliable ones." She crossed her fingers.

If he heard doubt in her voice, he let it go, switched gears. "How was your blind date?"

"No comment."

"That bad?"

She blew on her tea.

"What happened? He make a pass at you?"

She leveled a look at him. "By *pass*, do you mean did he grab my ass in the foyer of the restaurant?"

"That would definitely be a pass."

"Then no, he didn't."

His pickle snapped when he bit it. "So what was the problem? Too tall? Too short? Too bald?"

She snorted. "Women aren't as shallow as men, you know." Well, not *as* shallow.

"Is that so? Because sometimes it seems like they only care about one thing."

"Sex?" She smirked. "No, wait. That would be men."

"Money."

She cocked her head. "Are women stalking you for your millions?"

He poked his salad. "What's he do for a living?"

"He's a lawyer."

"A rich one?"

"Probably."

His head came up, eyes narrowed, studying her face. "But you're not interested?"

"I walked out and left him in the restaurant. Does that answer your question?"

"Yeah, I guess it does." He sounded pleased, which stupidly made her glad she'd told him.

Then he forked a cherry tomato into his mouth. Bit into it, and damn it, she could almost feel the squirt.

Why in the world is that so sexy? Why do I want to lick the juice off his tongue?

She locked her jaw, made herself look anywhere but at his lips. And she decided that Leo Payne had been right about one thing.

Cherry tomatoes *were* the most dangerous vegetable.

Chapter Five

CODY DROPPED A hundred on the table. "Where we headed first?"

Julie blinked liked she'd forgotten why they were there. Then she dug out her phone. Tapped and scrolled, all business.

"I've got two places in Beacon Hill, another in the North End. All walking distance to Mass General. Close to bars and restaurants. Nice routes to run along the waterfront or the Charles."

"Sounds good." He stood up, looked meaningfully down at his still-splotchy jeans.

She bit her lip. "I suppose you'll want to change."

"Uh-huh. Come up with me?"

"Not happening."

"I promise not to seduce you." He crossed his fingers behind his back. "I'm just afraid you'll disappear again."

"I'm not going anywhere. I've invested too much time

in you. I want a sale." She pulled her boots on. The zipping noise went straight to his cock. Christ, even soaking wet she made him hard. He turned away. "Don't you want your change?" she called after him.

"It's Christmas," he said over his shoulder.

She caught up to him at the door. He held her coat for her, got another whiff of her hair, a citrusy scent that ramped up his arousal. He turned away to fiddle with his own jacket, pretended the zipper was stuck so he could keep his back to her for a minute. Christ, he was like a high schooler with a boner in front of the class.

When he had himself together, he found her checking her email.

"Done primping?" she smirked.

"Just bracing for your Boston weather." He pushed open the door. The rain had morphed to snow. Half an inch already coated the parked cars. The pewter sky had turned so dark the streetlights were on, though it wasn't yet three o'clock.

"Back in Texas we see snow once in a blue moon," he went on, "and it doesn't last." He turned up his collar, reminded himself to buy some damn gloves. "But I'm betting on a white Christmas here."

"That would be nice," she said, but without much enthusiasm.

Back at the Plaza, he tried once more to lure her upstairs. She gave him the fish-eye, plunked down in one of the ornate lobby chairs, and pulled out her phone instead.

In his room, he didn't pause for a shower, though he was chilled to the bone. Sure, she'd promised to stay put, but she was unpredictable. Pistol hot one minute, glacier cold the next. Hard then soft, stern then sexy. Hell, she was all over the map, and he was damned if he could figure what made her shoot off in which direction and why.

But he *wanted* to figure it out. An hour over lunch had convinced him of that. The blind dates, the psychic dream-house thing. All of it.

And he wanted her in bed too.

He added a hoodie under his jacket and was downstairs in ten minutes. Breathed a sigh of relief that she was still where he left her, phone to her ear, eyes rolled to the ceiling, her pained expression all about forbearance for whatever she was hearing.

Crossing the lobby toward her, his chest got tight, and he almost laughed out loud at his own perversity. Typically, he went for the big-titted blondes most guys panted for, but Julie appealed to him on another plane entirely. She was pretty, all right, but she was more than that. She seemed . . . wholesome.

Wholesome. Now that was a word he ordinarily would've swallowed like medicine. But on her, it looked good. Go figure.

The chandeliers sparked off the red in her hair. Her crossed leg swung like a black leather metronome. Strolling up to her, he stopped a little too close to her chair. Call him a caveman, but he liked it when she looked up at him.

She said a quick goodbye and shut off her phone.

"Trouble?" he asked.

She stood up, swinging her purse so it slapped him in the nuts. A brush-back, not an accident.

"Just my nosy, interfering sister grilling me about my date." She headed for the door at the same half run she'd used to get out of the weather. It occurred to him that it was her customary speed.

He lagged behind. After twelve straight in the ER, he wasn't moving at anybody's pace but his own.

"She the one who set you up?" he said.

She stopped to wait for him, just aggravated enough to talk about it. "Why does she care if *I* have a date for *her* wedding? She's the only one who needs a date!"

She started for the door again. He lagged behind. She stopped, in a huff. "Are you injured or something? Did you sprain an ankle running in those boots?"

He pulled up alongside her. "I didn't know we were in a race. But remember, the tortoise beats the hare."

She rolled her eyes, shoved open the door. "I was planning to take the T to Park Street and then walk, but at this rate, we need a cab."

The doorman signaled for one, and they slid into the backseat. Cody made sure to spread his legs wide so his knee rubbed against hers. She scooted closer to the door.

"Beacon Hill," she told the driver. To Cody, "We might as well write off the North End. We'll never make it before dark." She shot him a speaking look.

He slid down in his seat, getting comfortable. He was happy to drag it out. Maybe talk her into dinner.

Maybe talk her into bed.

The sky had gone even darker, showing off the Christmas lights along Boylston Street. Candles glowed in windows, colored lights framed doorways and curled around handrails. They cut down Charles Street between the Public Garden and the Common, where long strands of lights in red, white, and green looped through the trees. The fresh snow made it magical, a Christmas card come to life.

Predictably, it made Cody sad. He wanted someone to share it with. Someone who wanted to share it with him.

Then Julie pointed to a retriever throwing a trail of snow as it streaked across the Common. It scooped up a bright blue ball, tore back to a woman in a purple coat, then joyfully eluded her when she tried for it.

"Does Betsy like to fetch?"

"Loves it. She's all dog, and fast as a bullet. Runs circles around me."

She laughed. "A snail could run circles around you."

He feigned hurt feelings. "I'll have you know I was a track star in high school. College too."

"Uh huh. And I was prom queen."

"You were?" He acted surprised. Squinted at her in the fading light. "I guess I can see it."

She whacked his arm.

They turned right on Beacon Street. She stopped the driver at the corner of Walnut. "It's easier to walk from here," she told Cody. Then, when he dawdled around to watch the ice skaters at the rink on the Common, she gazed regretfully after the taillights. "Maybe I spoke too soon."

"Maybe you need to slow down." He dragged out his

drawl, tipped his head at the rink. "Never seen folks skate outdoors before."

"Oh. Right." She seemed to settle down, willing to give him his moment.

He took it. Soaked up the colored lights, the music. The snow had picked up while they rode in the cab. Even in this weather, people lined up to get on the ice.

He looked away from the skaters to lock eyes with Julie. Fat flakes settled on her hair, a glitter effect. A big one caught on her lashes, and his chest tightened again. It must be all this Christmas stuff that was making him maudlin. He had to clear his throat to speak.

"What's the hurry, anyway?

"The hurry is that I'm trying to show you two condos in"—she broke eye contact first, checked her watch—"less than two hours." She set off at a clip, crossing Beacon Street, heading up Walnut.

He took his time following. "How long can it take to look at two condos anyway?" he called ahead.

She stopped to wait. "At your pace, a week."

He caught up. "You seem to know this neighborhood."

"It's my job to know neighborhoods. But you're right, I know this one better than most. My place is a few streets over that way."

"No shit?" That got his blood pumping. They could be neighbors. Friends.

Friends with benefits.

Suddenly he wanted to see where she lived. The place she called home. When she started moving in the other direction, he said, innocently, "You should get out of those damp clothes."

Her step hitched. It had to be tempting. "You don't want to get sick." He did the smile. "Doctor's orders."

Whoa. She spun on him. "I don't need a *doctor* telling me what to do. Stick your advice—" She bit off the rest, started to push on.

"Julie. Honey." He picked up his pace, touched a hand to her arm. "Whatever I said, I take it back. I just thought you'd want to be comfortable."

She shook off his hand, but she came to a stop, thought about it while her breath fogged the cold air. Then she nodded once. "Yes. I want to be comfortable." She one-eightied. He trailed behind, deciding it was even harder keeping up with her brain than her body.

Her street was narrow, the sidewalks practically non-existent. But the houses, they were beautiful. Brick, as old as any in the country. Hitching posts and boot scrapers by the front door. Some with a narrow drive leading back to a carriage house. To a Texas boy, it was as foreign as Mars.

"This is nice," Cody said, knowing it for an understatement but hard pressed to describe how he felt. Like even though he'd never set foot here before, never imagined such a place, he was coming home.

Cutting between two red brick houses with wreaths on their doors, Julie led him down a driveway to the brick carriage house at the end. The downstairs had been converted to a one-car garage with an arched doorway and authentic-looking green wooden door. Beside it, the regular entry door had a glass pane, but no wreath.

She unlocked the door, left it open behind her. He took it as an invitation, stomping his boots on the mat inside. Stairs rose directly before him, bringing him to another door. She'd left that one ajar too. Leaving his snowy jacket on a hook, he toed off his boots and stepped into her personal space.

A hundred years ago, it was a hayloft, stinking of manure. Now, it smelled like gingerbread. And it was snug, with painted plaster walls, exposed beams, recessed lighting. Through large, modern windows he saw the snow falling outside, but in here it was all thick rugs and warm colors.

The room wasn't huge, but it felt spacious, with a modern kitchen at one end, set off from the living area by an island topped with dark granite. At the other end of the room, a gas fireplace was framed in the same stone. A plush sofa reigned before it, calling to him. The long night dragged at his frame.

He heard drawers thumping in a room behind the kitchen, probably her bedroom. He'd like to see where she slept. If she had a king-sized bed. A fluffy down comforter. A drawer full of sex toys.

But moseying back there would get him thrown out on his ear, and since he never wanted to leave, he went for the sofa instead.

The upholstery was suede-y, just as soft as it looked. The pillowy cushions cradled him like a bosom. It took everything he had not to prop his feet on the coffee table.

As he sank into the couch, every minute of his twelve-hour shift settled into his bones. He stared blindly at his reflection in the fireplace glass. His lids weighed a thousand pounds each.

"The fireplace remote's on the end table." Julie's voice seemed to come from a long way away. With a hand as heavy as a brick, he found it. A faint beep, then the flames leapt to life.

The next minute, it seemed, she was peering down at him, wearing jeans and a snuggly sweater the same moss green as her eyes. He blinked. Slowly and with great effort.

She made a tsking sound.

He tried to smile, but his head fell back. A groan slipped out.

He quit fighting and let himself go.

JULIE GLARED AT Cody as a snore issued forth.

"Hey." She rocked his shoulder. "Hey. Cody. Wake up."

No response, just another snore. He was out cold. Dead to the world.

What was she supposed to do now?

She tiptoed to the kitchen. Paced a circle. Chewed her nails. His masculine presence threw her whole space out of whack. It threw *her* out of whack. Testosterone wafted off him like the aroma of bacon.

Who could say no to bacon?

She had to get rid of him before she did something stupid. But how? She couldn't carry him down to a cab. He weighed two hundred pounds if he weighed an ounce.

Besides, she felt sorry for him. Sort of. He'd worked all night . . .

No. This was *his* fault. She fisted her hips. If he hadn't pestered her, he'd be in bed at the Plaza and she'd be wrapped in seaweed at the spa.

Vowing to wake him, she marched to the sofa, then froze up at the sight of his big body, relaxed and defenseless. The intimacy of it tore at her heart. She hadn't seen a man sleep since David closed his eyes in her arms.

She retreated to the kitchen to hyperventilate.

Maybe she'd let him sleep for a while. Just a catnap while she kept her distance. Pouring Cap'n Crunch, she parked on a stool at the island to eat it, then realized she was chewing quietly, and kicked herself. Damn it, she hadn't asked him to cork off on her sofa!

Deliberately, she clanked her spoon on her bowl.

Then she felt bad about it. After all, he was her guest.

And so it went for an hour, as she seesawed between outrage and empathy. She knew very well she was being ridiculous, overreacting to having a man in her space. But it unsettled her on a cellular level.

After David died, she'd sold their dream house—through another Realtor—and moved into this carriage house directly behind it. The renovations had taken six months. Since then, no man had set foot in this space. It was hers. Her refuge.

Here, she could torture herself in peace, watching from the front window as another couple enjoyed what should have been her happy home. They didn't seem to realize it wasn't their dream house. They were too busy outfitting the nursery for the baby.

Now, as the minutes stretched and the man on her

sofa snored peacefully, the knots inside her tied tighter. She stewed and she paced. She damn near wrung her hands. And yet she felt powerless to act. Powerless to wake him and chase him out; powerless to stop wanting to jump him; powerless to forget about him and go watch *Dr. Phil.*

She was considering a Valium when her doorbell chimed. She jumped a foot. Leaping to the door, she opened it soundlessly and sprinted down the steps in her socks.

Night had fallen. Her outside lamps had come on, and through the glass she saw Amelia waiting in the falling snow, a cookie tin in her mittened hands.

Swearing, Julie flattened herself to the wall. She couldn't let her sister inside. If Amelia saw Cody, she'd get all kinds of ideas. Julie would never hear the end of it.

Could she pretend she wasn't home?

She peeked out again. Amelia was studying the upstairs windows. She'd never give up as long as the lights were on.

Sure enough, she reached for the bell again. Julie whipped the door open. "Hi. I was napping." She faked a yawn.

Amelia barged past her, not taking the hint. "I thought you might be. I've been calling your cell."

"Sorry, I muted it for the closing." Julie got in front of her before she hit the stairs. "I was just going out."

Amelia's brows shot up. "I thought you were sleeping."

"Well, I was resting up to go out. Now."

Amelia grinned. "With Leo? You're going out again

already?" She elbowed past Julie, steamed up the stairs. "I was hoping you'd like him. His sister's a doll."

Julie sprinted past to cut her off at the landing. Lowered her voice to a whisper. "Shh, I've got a soufflé in the oven. The slightest noise can make it drop. Even a change in air pressure. We shouldn't open the door."

Amelia put a hand on her hip. "What's going on, Jules? Why don't you want me inside?" Then her eyes lit up. "My present's in there, isn't it? It's too big to wrap!"

And shoving the cookies at Julie, she pushed her aside and charged in.

AMELIA TURNED IN a circle, scanning for her present. The treadmill she wanted? The antique bureau she'd been hemming and hawing over since her birthday?

Nope. Everything looked like it always did. No presents in sight. Not a single Christmas decoration.

And then—wait a minute—she zeroed in on a tawny mop of hair poking over the sofa. Adding one and one, she got two, and shooting Julie a wide-eyed look, she zoomed over to see who it was.

Julie caught up to her before she could blare out a greeting. "He's sleeping!" she hissed, and tried to drag Amelia away. But Amelia didn't budge.

Instead, she stared, rapt, at the long-legged Adonis sprawled on her sister's sofa. His arms had fallen open; so had his knees. His lashes fanned out on tanned cheekbones. She raked her eyes from his messy hair to his white gym socks and back up again for good measure.

Whoa.

"This is *Leo*?" she whispered, hardly believing her eyes. He was sex-dream material, tall and rangy, with snug jeans that left nothing to the imagination. Hardcore erotica on the hoof.

"Believe me, it's not Leo," Julie whispered back.

"Then who is he?" she hissed. "I want deets!"

"There *are* no deets." Julie's beet-red face gave the lie to her words. "He's a client. Looking at places in Beacon Hill."

"Baloney. He's looking at the inside of his eyelids." Amelia bore in. "What's going on? You never bring clients here. And where's his wife?" She sucked a breath, her whisper rising. "Are you having an affair with a client?"

"Will you *stop*?" Julie hauled her away from the sofa.

Amelia went along with her as far as the kitchen. Then she dug in her heels, worry sharpening her tone. "Julie, tell me right now. Is he married?"

"For God's sake, he's single, all right? We stopped here so I could change out of my wet clothes. He fell asleep while I was in the bedroom." She fisted her hair. "I've been angsting for an hour, wondering if I should wake him up, or let him sleep, or what the hell else I should do with him."

Amelia homed in on the operative fact. "He's single? You never work with singles."

Julie rolled her eyes. "There's a first time for everything."

"And your first time happens to be Mr. Six-Foot Tenderloin?" She grinned at Julie. "Did you do it yet?"

"Do what?" Julie truly looked confused, but she could be faking it.

"Have sex, dummy."

Julie's fair skin went redder. "I can't believe you."

Amelia sighed, disappointed. She'd never asked outright, but she was pretty sure Julie hadn't been with another man in three years. David's illness, his death, all of it was a tragedy, and her heart bled for her sister. But it was past time for her to move on. And this guy seemed like he might be the ticket.

One way to find out.

Reaching out, she took the cookie tin from Julie's hand, held it at arm's length. And let go.

It clanged like a bell when it hit the floor. The hunk shot to his feet and spun around to face them, obviously befuddled. His single-malt eyes blinked, trying to focus. Then one hand plowed his hair, the other went to his fly, and Amelia broke into a grin. Did he really think they'd taken advantage of him?

Well, he *had* looked delicious snoozing on the sofa.

On his feet, he shaped up even better. Broad shoulders, narrow hips. Amelia considered herself a connoisseur; she'd taken years to settle down. And this guy was all that, and more.

Then he smiled. Oh lord. The world tilted on its axis. The moon and the sun rose at once. She looked at Julie. Her sister stared at him like a deer in the headlights.

At last, she thought. *Oh Julie, at last.*

Crushing gingerbread under her feet, she crossed the

room at warp speed. "I'm Julie's sister, Amelia," she said, reaching for his hand.

"Cody Brown," he said, and she nearly swooned at his drawl. Could he possibly get any hotter?

She smiled her friendliest smile. "It sounds like you're a long way from home, Cody."

"About two thousand miles."

Julie popped up beside her, clamped a hand on her arm. Amelia sensed her rising panic. Julie knew what she was up to.

"I'll bet you'd like a home-cooked meal," Amelia rushed on. "And it just so happens that I'm doing lasagna tomorrow." She ignored the fingers drilling her biceps. "It's a family thing. We get together every weekend. We'd love it if you'd join us."

Cody's eyes tracked to Julie. "It's been all restaurants and room service since I got to Boston," he spun out in that delectable drawl. "Home cooking sounds inviting."

Amelia risked a glance at Julie. She'd locked eyes with Cody, a silent communication that read threats on one side and taunts on the other.

Then his gaze tracked back to her, and Amelia caught her breath. Full lips, crinkly eyes. And that dimple. Oh my.

"What can I bring?" he asked her. "And don't say 'nothing.' A Texan never shows up empty-handed."

"Wine's always welcome," she got out, still recovering from the smile. "We go through lots of it." She peeled off Julie's fingers, which had fused to her arm. "We eat at two, but come anytime. Julie usually shows up around one. Why don't you come along with her?"

Making tracks for the door, she glanced over her shoulder. They looked perfect together, Cody's powerful frame alongside Julie's willowy build, firelight flickering behind them. Amelia's heart squeezed. In three days, she'd be married to the love of her life. More than anything, she wanted the same happiness for Julie.

Closing the door behind her, she smiled to herself. Maybe she'd been right after all. Maybe her Christmas present *had* been waiting inside.

A mouthwatering cowboy with a knee-buckling smile. And a brand new start for her sister.

Chapter Six

JULIE GLARED AT Cody. "Seriously?"

He shrugged. "How could I refuse?"

"Like this: 'No thank you, I have plans.'"

"But I don't. Unless you want to show me some more condos."

"*More*? We haven't seen *one* yet. You were too busy taking a beauty nap on my sofa."

"Why didn't you wake me up?"

"Because." She crossed her arms.

He tilted his head. "Because I'm so cute when I'm asleep?"

"Because you're quiet when you're asleep. You're not prodding and pestering and propositioning me."

He let out a startled chuckle. "Julie, honey, you must have me confused with somebody else. I'm the most easygoing man you'll ever meet."

"Oh please." She stalked to the kitchen, started sweeping up cookie crumbs. "Anyway, it's dark out, and it's snowing, and it's Friday night. It's too late to go looking at condos. You can go home now."

He didn't want to go home. He wanted to stay here, with her. But for once in his silver-tongued life, words failed him. He couldn't summon the magic that might persuade her to share a meal with him, if not her bed.

He stared into the fire, dwelling on the irony. He'd finally found a woman who wasn't impressed by his MD, and she didn't want anything to do with him.

"Why are you here?" she asked, breaking into his thoughts. "Why'd you come to Boston?"

He looked over at her. She was leaning on the broom, watching him with curious eyes. He must have looked pathetic, because she stood the broom in the corner, brought him a Coke from the fridge. "I'd give you a beer, but you'd keel over. Then I'd never get you out of here."

He tried for a smile as he accepted the Coke. She pushed his chest, a light shove that invited him to sit. He took her up on it.

She sat on the coffee table facing him. "So. Why are you here?"

He wet his throat with some Coke. "In six weeks, I'll take over as head of Emergency Medicine. Right now I'm cycling myself through every shift in the ER, learning the place inside and out."

Her jaw tightened. "Couldn't you do the same thing in Texas?" she asked, like she wished he'd get on the next plane back there.

"Probably. But then I'd be in Texas. Boston's as far away as I could get."

As soon as he said it, he bit his tongue. Now she'd ask why he wanted out of Texas.

He wasn't ready to talk about it, so he changed the subject. Pointed his chin at a photograph on the mantle: A good-looking guy with wire-rimmed glasses sitting in a coffee shop, Julie standing behind him with her arms looped around his neck. Both of them smiled happily at the camera.

"Who's that?" he asked, hoping it was her brother.

She looked over her shoulder at the photo, sorrow sliding across her features like a cloud passing over the sun. "That's David. My fiancé."

"You're engaged?" *What about the blind dates? The smokin' hot lip-lock in the restaurant?*

Then she said, "Not anymore. He died."

"Shit. I'm sorry." He shifted uncomfortably because, to his shame, he was also relieved. To make up for it, he added, "Looks like a nice guy."

"His heart was as big as the world." She brought her hands together in her lap, looked down at them. "He worked with at-risk kids. Kids whose parents were druggies, or dead, or in jail. Kids with the odds stacked against them. He did nothing but good in this world. It was a better place while he was in it."

She twisted her ring, and Cody realized it was a diamond. A puny one. David hadn't had much money, but Julie didn't care.

He thought of the iceberg Bethany had picked out,

big enough to sink the Titanic, and the old humiliation soured his stomach. He'd actually believed she loved him. What a sucker. No sooner had he foolishly proposed than she'd dragged him to Austin's finest jeweler, where she rejected stone after stone, explaining that she absolutely *had* to have a bigger diamond than her sister, who'd married a mere stockbroker, and a *much* bigger diamond than her BFF, who'd settled for a paltry lawyer.

She, Bethany Mills, was going to be a *doctor's* wife. She'd landed the biggest fish, so she should have the biggest diamond.

That night, just for the hell of it, he told her he'd always wanted to teach kindergarten and now that he had her love and support, he planned to quit medicine and follow his dream.

By morning, he was single again.

He was also hurt. So hurt that when Bethany hooked up with a colleague a few months later, the long-standing offer from Mass General started looking mighty good.

And that was the ignominious story behind his move to Boston. He'd gotten his heart broken and run away like a girl.

He wasn't ready to share it with Julie. Which wasn't a problem because she wasn't paying attention to him anyway. In fact, she was a million miles away, and he had the awful feeling that if he didn't do something to bring her back, she'd keep drifting and he'd lose her for good. He didn't want that to happen.

He set the empty can on the coffee table. "I'm sure he

was proud of you too. It's a nice little niche you carved for yourself, the whole dream-house angle."

Her brows scrunched. "It's not an *angle*. I told you before, it's what I do. I don't care if you believe me or not, but I actually have a talent for it."

He nodded agreeably. "You must. 'Cause if you always farted around like you did this afternoon, you'd be out of business."

Her spine stiffened. Her gaze sharpened. And she was right back where he wanted her, focused on him like a laser.

"The farting around," she clipped, "is on you. First you were hungry. Then wet. Then sleepy. You're worse than a baby. At least with a baby, I could change his diaper, stick a bottle in his mouth, and let him nap in the stroller while I went about my business. But you, you killed the whole afternoon."

He faked offended. "I'll take the hit for lunch, but I gotta remind you, we're only here because you were wet too." He spread his hands. "Now, if it was up to me, we'd have both stripped down and warmed up by the fire—"

She held up a hand. "Why are you still here?"

"You want me to leave?"

She nodded vigorously. "Yes, please."

"Got another blind date?"

She stood up. "I have things to do."

"Such as?"

"Such as none of your beeswax."

He threw out some chum. "Me, I was thinking of taking in a movie."

"Good idea. Maybe the hotel has in-room porn." She shooed him with her hands.

He took his sweet time, ambling toward the door like it was his own idea. Like he wasn't being thrown out on his ear.

He pulled on his boots while she tapped her foot. Shrugged into his coat as she held the door. Smiled an innocent smile and said, "So what time should I come by?"

Her jaw dropped. "You're not serious. You don't really want to come to dinner."

"I told your sister I'd be there, so I'll be there." He cocked his head. "That make you nervous?"

She sputtered. "Oh please. Irritable, yes. Nervous, no."

"So what time should I come by?"

He could hear her teeth grind. He bit back another smile.

"She's right around the corner," she got out at last. "Just come whenever."

"Okay then, I'll see you at noon."

"*What*? No! One o'clock is early enough." She put a hand on his back, gave him a shove through the door. "You can get a cab on Beacon." And she closed it behind him.

As he stepped out into the snow, he made himself look ahead instead of back. He didn't want to see the warm lights he was leaving behind, and if she wasn't watching him walk away, he didn't want to know it.

What he did want was to get inside her defenses. She was prickly as a hedgehog, but whenever he snuck past her quills, he found something interesting. Like the psychic dream-house thing. That was just weird enough to be true.

And her smidgen of a diamond. That *really* got to him. That, and her sorrow. They put his own hurt feelings to shame. Made him see what he should've seen months ago, that Bethany had wounded his pride, not broken his heart. Hell, he'd hardly thought of her since he hit Boston a week ago. Only once or twice since meeting Julie, and then Bethany suffered by comparison.

He shoved his cold hands deeper into his pockets as he turned downhill toward the Common. Along the sidewalk, old-fashioned streetlamps glowed. Brick row houses marched along both sides of the street, each one decorated for Christmas with wreaths and candles and swags of white lights.

Julie had none of those things. No tree shining from her window. No holiday spirit at all. It was bound up inside her, like everything else. Like her passion and laughter and heart.

Julie Marone, he decided, was a package that needed unwrapping.

Well, it was Christmas, right?

Julie sank down on her sofa. Rolled her head to the side and took one long, delicious sniff of pure male pheromones.

Why was she torturing herself? Cody was a *doctor*, for God's sake. She shouldn't be so attracted to him.

But she was, damn it. She was.

She scraped her fingers over her scalp, tugged her hair back till it stretched her whole face. Dinner would be an ordeal. He'd charm the socks off her family. Amelia practically drooled when she saw him asleep on the sofa. Her mother would go down just as hard, and when she got a load of his drawl, forget about it.

They'd shove him down her throat with both hands. And she was terrified that she'd give in and swallow.

Her gaze strayed to David's photo. His gentle eyes. His peaceful smile. Even during his illness he'd been a calm, steadying presence. A counterpoint to her fly-off-the-handle temper, her raging impatience and burning resentment at a world where death chose its victims without rhyme or reason, where goodness was irrelevant and suffering came to those who deserved it least.

Yes, David fought his battle with dignity and grace, while she beat her fists bloody against the injustice of it all.

And when it was over and David's ashes had washed out with the tide, still the furnace of her fury roared. Grief stoked it; so did loneliness and impotence and guilt. Unable to accept her loss, she turned her silent wrath on the doctors who'd failed to save him. On all doctors everywhere who went home to their expensive houses and their pampered spouses while David, her David, drifted out to sea.

For three years that fire had burned in her breast, unquenched by time, impervious to reason. Now Cody threatened the very underpinning, her absolute belief that doctors cared about nothing but money. Because he simply didn't fit the frame.

She wanted him to. Oh, how she wanted him to. But

she knew the money was in specialties, like surgery and oncology to name a dastardly few. It wasn't in emergency medicine. And pumping out a junkie's stomach or patching up a battered wife didn't make for glamorous cocktail conversation.

Thanks to Cody, she had to consider that maybe, just maybe, some doctors actually cared about helping people. Which meant that if she'd looked harder, maybe she could have found one. Someone who could have saved David.

But wouldn't that put his death on *her*?

Oh God. She couldn't go there.

She wouldn't.

Chapter Seven

THE DOORBELL CHIMED at one o'clock sharp. Julie's stomach fluttered in spite of herself. Stomping on the butterflies, she took her time pulling on a parka and mittens, then descended the stairs at a measured pace.

She opened the door, her lips schooled into a frown. And there he stood, all six-foot-sexy of him filling out his ass-hugging jeans and battered leather jacket, looking for all the world like he'd galloped in off the range to ride roughshod over the bluebloods of Boston.

Those stupid spurs jangled in her head again. Her palms popped a sweat in her mittens. She fought his hotness with all her might.

Then he dimpled up. His whiskey eyes crinkled. And the butterflies squirted out from under her boot and did a happy dance in her stomach. Before she could stop it, she broke out in a smile, stepped toward him as if she expected him to kiss her.

Which he did. Oh yes, he dropped his chin and laid his warm lips on hers, kept them there, and it wasn't a hey-it's-nice-to-see-you kiss. No, this was a let's-go-inside-and-get-naked kiss. It seared her lips, spreading out from there like flame consuming paper, eating away the resistance she'd drummed into her brain, lighting up every cell, every sinew.

Her mittens slid over his shoulders. His arms closed around her. Out of her head flew all her inhibitions. Her parka rode up; she felt his heat on her belly, soaking through her sweater. His cock, hard and heavy, defied their layers, scorching her skin through denim and wool. She parted her lips, taking his tongue, giving him hers, letting them dance the dance that their bodies demanded.

He cupped her ass in one bare hand, slid the other up her back, inside her shirt, under her bra. His thumb brushed the curve of her breast and both of them moaned. He shoved her bra up, took her weight in his palm. Her breast seemed to swell, overflowing his hand. He thumbed her nipple. Her legs tried to buckle.

He dragged his lips across her cheek. Scraped his teeth down her jaw. "Inside," he murmured, breath hot on her throat, "take me inside."

Inside.

Inside her house. Inside her body.

Inside her defenses. Inside her heart.

Fear trumped passion. "I can't," she said, and took a step back. He opened his arms and released her.

Embarrassed for reasons she couldn't even identify, she turned away from him, yanking off her mittens, adjusting her bra with sweaty fingers. In the glass pane of the door, she saw his reflection. The hunger in his eyes, the disappointment on his face.

"I'm sorry," she said past the lump in her throat.

He caught her gaze in the glass, gave a rueful half smile. "Should've kept my mouth shut. We could've done it right here in the snow. I wouldn't have minded."

She tried to smile back at him, the kind of smile that would gently tell him she took responsibility for letting things go too far, and at the same time push him away, back into the role she'd assigned him.

But the smile wouldn't come. She was practically paralyzed, confounded by emotions that just wouldn't jibe. She hated that he was a doctor, but loved how funny and kind and incredibly generous he was. He scared her down to her DNA, made her doubt rock-solid beliefs, but she wanted to strip off her clothes and rub against him like a pussycat.

She couldn't process it. She didn't want to try. She wanted to go back inside, pour a glass of wine, and watch *CSI* reruns until she went numb.

Mostly, she wanted him to go away and leave her in peace. As usual, he wasn't cooperating.

As if to make the point, he said, "You don't mind helping me pick out the wine, do you?" He wiggled the fingers that had almost undone her. "No gloves yet, so I didn't want to carry it all the way from Back Bay."

Damn his drawl. She unzipped her parka. Flapped it a few times, then zipped it halfway. "There's a wine store on the way," she said, sticking her sweaty hands back into her mittens and setting off down the driveway with her usual rapid stride. "You can't go wrong with a mid-range cab or Chianti. We're all about red in my family."

Then she realized she was talking to thin air. She should've remembered that evolution moved faster than Cody.

She pulled up and waited while he crawled up to join her, then set off again, trying to moderate her pace. But no matter how slow she walked, he fell behind.

He ambled. He sauntered. A snail could have outrun him.

She simply *could not* walk that slow.

Half a block down, she threw up her hands. "Are you sure you work in the ER?" She pictured a trauma patient bleeding out while he strolled to the gurney.

"The hectic pace suits me."

"You're kidding."

"I'm greased lightning in the ER."

"You're frozen molasses now."

He smiled. She turned her back on his dimple, strode ahead. "The store's right around the corner. We should be there by nightfall."

His laugh rumbled behind her. He had a great laugh, deep and sudden, like she'd surprised it out of him. She had to get away from it. It was too warm, too tempting. She hit the gas and left him to follow at his own glacial pace.

When he came through the door, she pushed two bottles into his hands. "These'll do."

He scanned the labels. "Uh-uh." He moved past her down the aisle.

She trailed after him. "What do you mean, uh-uh? What's wrong with them?"

"Not a thing." He propped them back on the shelf, reached for their pricier classico cousins.

She puffed up. "They're perfectly acceptable mid-range wines."

He headed for the register. She trailed after him. He paid. She simmered.

Out on the sidewalk, she went at him again. "I can't believe you spent a hundred bucks on two bottles of chianti to drink with my sister's lasagna. Who're you trying to impress? Just because you're a *doctor* with money coming out of your ears—"

He whirled at a speed that had her blinking, stuck his face down in hers, and gave her both barrels. "That's right, I'm a *doctor*! And you're the only woman in America who thinks that's a bad thing!" He pulled back, insult all over his face. "As for money, I guaran-damn-tee you make more than I do. And without the loans to pay off, either."

Then he gave her his back, took off at double his normal pace. After a few beats, she found her voice.

"Hey. Cody. You're going the wrong way."

CODY MADE A show of stomping back to her. "I'm surprised you didn't let me wander away." He said it tartly, letting her know she'd rubbed his fur the wrong way.

"Amelia would've sent out a search party." There was an apology in her smile. And an olive branch.

Fat chance. It's not that easy, sister.

"I don't doubt you could've talked her out of it," he said. "Convinced her I'm an asshole. I'm sure you could sell it."

"You're many things, Cody, but you're not an asshole." She sounded almost regretful.

She set off down Mount Vernon Street. He didn't try to keep up. She stopped at the corner, visibly swallowed her impatience. At least she felt bad enough not to nag him into a sprint.

He cut her some slack, gave her a smile that turned her cheeks pinker than the cold. She was mule-headed, mercurial, downright impossible to please, and he was tired of getting squeezed into that tiny box she'd built for him. But the truth was, if she fucked like she kissed, he wasn't going anywhere.

Besides, when she let down her guard, he wanted to eat her up.

"Those condos you lined up for me," he said when he reached her, "they around here?"

"Within a few blocks."

"So we'll be neighbors."

She shrugged, but with discomfort, not indifference. "I guess. Not that people see much of each other here. Lots of professionals."

"They all travel at light speed like you?"

That got a laugh out of her. She had a great laugh. It rolled up from her belly, rising a register along the way. Too bad she hoarded it like gold.

"I'm serious," he said. "You'd be arrested for speeding in Texas. Mowing innocent folks down on the sidewalk."

She laughed again, and his chest swelled. He liked to make people laugh, but he'd never felt *proud* of it before. He caught her hand, hooked it through his arm. "This'll slow you down," he said. When she shied, he clamped it to his side. "Might speed me up too," he offered. "You never know."

"There's not far to go." She pointed at a brick house across the street. Red shutters, lace curtains, and candles in the windows.

"Their dream house?"

"Nope. That's in Natick. They're moving in after New Year's."

Amelia met them at the door, apron over her jeans. Now that he was awake, Cody saw she was as pretty as Julie, but more petite. Otherwise, they might almost have been twins if not for the hair. Amelia's was an eye-catching blonde, usually his favorite. But Julie's glossy chestnut was something special. It suited her, lush and fiery.

Amelia kissed his cheek like he was already family, raised her brows at the wine, then steered him into the living room where a Christmas tree glittered, a fire crackled on the hearth, and a very fine-looking woman who could only be Julie's mother came at him like a dog at a bone.

"You're Cody," she said, latching onto his large hand with both of her small ones. "I'm Ellen, and I'm so glad to meet you."

"Pleased to meet you too, ma'am," he said, and her eyes widened two sizes.

Amelia laughed. "I warned you, Mom. That drawl's deadly." She winked at Cody. "Come on out to the kitchen and you can open the wine. I'm dying to try it. It's ten points up from our usual."

Julie had disappeared toward the back of the house. Now he followed Amelia in that direction, Ellen tagging along. "So, Cody, Amelia says Julie's helping you find a place. She usually works with couples, you know. She must like you."

"I sure do hate to disagree with you, Ellen. But I think if you asked her, she'd tell you I roped her into it."

He smiled at her. She stumbled over the doorjamb.

Julie was already in the kitchen. Steadying her mother, she aimed a look at Cody that said to be careful where he pointed that thing. He fired one at her too. She sniffed, but her cheeks went rosy.

"Cody." Amelia pulled him toward the stove where a man half his size was lifting a tray of lasagna out of the oven. "This is Ray, my fiancé."

Ray threw him a grin as he maneuvered the tray onto a trivet. "I hear you're from Texas. My Dad's from out in the Hill Country."

"No kidding." Cody grinned too. "I grew up out there. My brother still runs the ranch."

Ray shed the potholders, stuck out his hand. "I bet my Dad could pin it down within five miles if he heard your drawl."

"Any real Texan could," Cody agreed.

Amelia pressed a bottle and corkscrew into his hand. Ellen set out six glasses. "My boyfriend's coming," she said, smiling up at him. "It's so nice that Julie won't be the odd man out again."

"Mom!" Julie hissed.

Cody popped the cork. Poured a swallow in one glass and passed it to Julie, smiling slyly. "She didn't approve of my choice," he whispered loudly to Ellen.

"I didn't *not* approve," Julie sputtered.

"Don't use double negatives, dear," Ellen said, then gave Cody an apologetic smile. "I'm a teacher for thirty years now, and still my children mangle the language."

Julie slugged the wine. "It's delicious, okay?" She held out her glass. Cody filled it. She guzzled half of it down.

"Jules," Amelia laughed, "you should savor that. You won't be getting it again unless Cody comes back." She gave Cody a wink that said he was welcome any time.

Ray clapped him on the shoulder. He had to reach up to do it. He couldn't be more than five foot six. "Amelia got me a new TV," he said. "My wedding gift. Come check it out."

They went down a short hall, into a small room that was all flat screen. Cody let out a whistle. "Sixty inches?"

"Sixty-five." Ray hit the power. The Patriots charged into the room, every pore on Tom Brady's face an inch wide. Ray waved him into a leather recliner with a built-in cup holder, took the other, and kicked out the leg rest. "Let's give the girls a minute to get you out of their systems."

"Uh-huh." Cody tipped back, crossed his boots at the ankle. "They're a good-looking bunch."

Ray nodded. "Uh-huh."

Then both of them groaned. Brady stalked off the field, disgusted. Cody tsked as the camera panned to Gisele. "Ol' Tom won't be getting any tonight."

They watched companionably while the Pats punted and the Giants ran it back to the thirty, then the fifty, then fumbled spectacularly.

Brady had just taken the field again when Amelia appeared in the doorway, hand on her hip. Both men dropped their leg rests in unison.

Ray was first on his feet. "Hi, honey. Just showing Cody the amazing, incredible, wonderful gift my beautiful, thoughtful, generous wife-to-be gave me." He planted a loud kiss on her cheek.

"Mmm-hmm." She tapped his chest. "The deal was that you'd DVR the game so we can watch it together."

"Oh, I am. It's recording. And I didn't look at the score. Honest."

Their affection was written all over them. Cody pushed past his envy. "You're a lucky man, Ray, marrying a fan."

"Julie's a fan too," Amelia said brightly. "She loves the Pats. She goes to a couple games every season."

Cody grinned. Himself, he wouldn't set foot in Gillette Stadium unless the Cowboys were playing, but he didn't have the heart to tell her.

The kitchen was aswirl, Ellen slicing bread, Julie making salad. Cody popped the cork on the other wine bottle, wishing he'd bought a case. He was completely at ease in this home, with these people. He liked them, and they seemed to like him too. Even Julie must feel how naturally he fit in, because she smiled at him when he topped off her glass. Didn't pull back when he laid a kiss on her cherry-red lips.

The doorbell chimed. Ellen ran for the door, came back a minute later with a guy who wouldn't see fifty for another ten years. Blond and built, his arm was locked around her waist.

"Cody, this is Jess. He's a personal trainer. *My* personal trainer." She gave Jess's biceps a squeeze. Then she paused. "Cody, Julie never mentioned what it is that you do."

"I'm a doctor," he said.

It fell like a brick.

Julie kept chopping, but the rest of them froze.

Everyone but Jess, who was oblivious to the chill in the room. "A doctor. Cool. What's your specialty?"

That brought Ellen to life. "For heaven's sake, we don't have to grill the poor man!" She shoved her wineglass into Jess's hand. "Drink this." He sipped obediently.

Amelia had gone whiter than chalk. "Oh, Jules," she said, brokenly. "I'm so sorry—"

"It's fine," Julie cut in, her tone closing the subject. She scraped cukes into the salad, set the knife in the sink. "I'm starving. Can we eat?"

Everyone sat down, but nobody ate. They passed the lasagna, then pushed it around with their forks. No one looked up. No one said a word.

Cody didn't know what to make of it. Sure, he knew Julie wasn't crazy about doctors. But this felt like a funeral. What the fuck?

Jess blundered cluelessly into the pall. "My cousin's a brain surgeon," he said. "*Bzzzzzz*"—he did a buzz saw—"right through the skull and into the old brainpan." He chortled a laugh. "Don't ask me how he does it, man. If I saw a brain, I'd faint like a sissy." He reached for the bread in the deafening silence. "How 'bout you, Cody? What's your gig?"

Cody glanced around the table, registered the speechless horror. Beside him, Julie's fingers twisted in her lap. And suddenly it all came together: the ring, the dead fiancé, the doctor phobia. Maybe malpractice had killed David. It wasn't unheard of.

He'd get the details later. For now he said to Jess, "I'm thinking about doing the marathon. Got any advice?"

It was exactly the right thing to distract him. Jess pointed a crust at him. "Got a deal going right now—a three-month training session geared for the marathon. We're a couple weeks into it, but I can prorate it for you." He gave Cody a once-over. "You look fit. Free weights or machines?"

Cody humored him with some details until Julie quit fiddling with her ring and took a bite of lasagna. That broke the ice. Everyone took a breath. The salad moved around the table, the wine too. Cody filled Julie's glass. She thanked him politely.

Ellen started talking about one of her problem students. Ray and Amelia chimed in, and the conversation flowed. Cody tuned it out, his attention all on Julie, her pale face and haunted eyes.

Taking the hand that still lay curled in her lap, he

linked his fingers with hers and gave a light squeeze. For a long, quiet moment, she didn't react. Then she took a sip of wine, swallowed like she had to push it past a sizeable lump, and offering him a tight-lipped smile, she gently but firmly extracted her hand.

He soldiered on through the meal, fielding questions about ranch life, asking some of his own, growing even fonder of Ellen and Amelia and the men they'd chosen. But all the while he was tuned to the quiet woman beside him, a ghost of the girl he'd made out with just hours before.

When it came time to clean up, he finagled his way into the kitchen with Amelia. Closing the door behind them, he cut to the chase. "What happened to David? How did he die?"

Amelia leaned a hip on the counter. "Brain cancer. A tumor the size of a lemon. Too involved to remove, too stubborn to radiate. Chemo didn't work either, just ruined the last weeks of his life."

Cody studied the floor tiles, played out the tragic scenario. Then, "She blames the docs, doesn't she?"

"Oh yeah." Amelia let out a sigh. "I know it's not rational. On some level she probably knows that too. But Cody, it was so awful. So brutal and painful and awful." Her throat caught. "I can't fault her. She had to do something with her anger. So she turned it on the doctors. Blamed them for failing him. For offering hope and delivering nothing but more pain."

A tear rolled down her cheek. She let it fall to the floor. "They were in love. Like Ray and me. They'd just bought their dream house." She looked up at him. "Now she walks past it every day. Stares through the windows at the couple living inside."

"You mean she can see it from her place?"

"It's the house right out front."

Cody's heart turned over. "She's torturing herself. Keeping the grief and the hate alive."

"I begged her to get counseling, but she refused. No more doctors, she said." Amelia huffed out a laugh. "I ended up going myself, trying to figure out how to help her."

She shrugged sadly. "All I really learned is that nobody can help her until she's ready to move on."

It was spitting snow when they left Amelia and Ray's, icy little slivers that glinted in the lamplight. Cody tucked Julie's hand under his arm. She didn't fight it.

The truth was, she appreciated the effort he'd made with her family. Even after Jess dropped a nuke on dinner, Cody had salvaged the meal. He'd wowed her mom and Amelia. Ray wanted to be besties. And Jess had a total man-crush on him. Who could blame them? Cody was perfect in every way but one.

But that one way was a deal breaker.

Now he poked along at his usual pace, while the snow mixed with sleet, pinging off the sidewalk. "Shouldn't Amelia be in a lather," he asked, "what with her wedding around the corner?"

Julie shrugged. "It's only twenty people. Just close

family." It still surprised her that Amelia hadn't wanted a blowout. She claimed it was the marriage, not the wedding, that mattered, but more likely she was sparing Julie the pomp and circumstance so she wouldn't dwell on the wedding David's death had denied her.

"Your Mom said you grew up in Newton."

"Mmm-hmm." She knew he was trying to make conversation, but dinner had drained her.

"Why'd you move to Beacon Hill?"

She tensed up. "I like it here."

"So do I," he said agreeably. "But there's nice places in Back Bay, closer to your office."

Why was he pushing this? Annoyed, she tried to pull her hand away. He clamped it to his side. The thrill of bulging biceps only made her tug harder.

"Julie, sweetheart, these boots weren't built for your Boston winter. I'm liable to land on my ass if you don't hold on to me."

"Oh." She quit tugging, tried to ignore his biceps as they inched along the sidewalk.

They were almost to her house when she realized her mistake. "We should've cut down to Beacon to get you a cab."

He kept moving down her driveway. "Not likely I'd let you walk home in the dark."

They paused outside her door. The scene of the kiss.

She detached her hand. Rubbed her arms like she was cold. She wasn't. She was never cold with Cody around.

What she was, was a mess. She needed time alone to wallow for a while. To dredge up her memories and nurse her grievances. Because—and she was ashamed to admit it—ever since Cody'd shown up in her life, David seemed to be slipping away. If she wasn't careful, she might forget how he'd suffered. How both of them suffered. And she'd promised herself never to forget. Or forgive.

He smiled. "Gonna invite me in for a drink?"

"I'm out of wine." She'd polished it off after booting him out last night.

"Actually, I was thinking about coffee."

"Oh." She tried to stay strong, but his smile beguiled her. "I have coffee."

He waited. Then, "Well? Can I have some?"

She wrestled the demon. Wanted to say yes. Struggled to say no.

She dragged her eyes away from his lips. Looked down at her mittens, and summoned the strength. "Listen, Cody. I can't get involved with you."

"Because I'm a doctor?"

"Yes."

"And you hate all doctors."

"Yes." It sounded ridiculous. But it was true. She studied the stitching on her thumb. Waited for him to say something, or leave, or be beamed up by aliens.

None of those things happened. Instead, the silence stretched until she had to look up. His smile was gone. Sleet peppered his cheek, but he looked too pissed to care. "I was in Texas when David died."

She bristled. "I don't expect you to understand."

"Try me."

"Why? So you can defend your species?"

"So I can figure out how to un-fuck-up your head."

It stung like a slap. She took a step back. Then fury leapt to her rescue, put a lash in her voice. "You arrogant ass. You're just like the rest, so sure you know best. Until it all goes to shit."

She whipped off a mitten, mimed a phone to her ear. "Sorry," she did a snotty secretary's nasal, "Dr. Know-It-All's at a conference in Vienna. He'll be back in March. Oh, you'll be dead by then? Sorry to hear that. I'll tell him you called."

Cody's eyes narrowed dangerously. His voice dropped to a growl. "I'm goddamned sick and tired of you and everybody else judging me by the degree on my wall. Back in the day, women used to want me—or not—for *who I am*. And mostly, they wanted me. Because I know how to have a good time. How to take things in stride. And except for politicians and serial killers, I don't dislike a person based on their job."

He was on a roll. "I got more going on than an MD, you know. I travel. I read. I play the bass. Hell, I rode the circuit for a year and got the buckle to prove it." He raked his hair back with both hands, vibrating frustration. "I'm wasting my time. It wouldn't matter to you if I won the Nobel Prize. You'll never see past your fucked-up-pig-headed-dumb-ass prejudice against doctors."

How dare he? How dare he belittle her feelings? How dare he judge her? She spiked a finger to his chest. "I don't need *you*, Dr. Brown, telling me what I should think or how I should feel. You don't know me. You don't know anything about me."

"I know more than you think. You're looking for someone to blame." He throttled back his anger. His voice came out hoarse. "You want to believe the docs didn't do everything they could, because otherwise you're gonna look at yourself, wonder if *you* did something wrong, or didn't do enough."

"You think you're so smart." Tears put an infuriating quaver in her voice. Then rage rose up to rescue her once more. She shoved his chest with both hands. "You don't know me! You don't know *anything*! So take your stupid smile and your stupid drawl and your stupid arrogant psychobabble *bullshit* and go back to your hotel and leave me alone!"

She got her key in the lock and stumbled inside, slammed the door behind her, and leaned back against it, trembling. If Cody tore it off the hinges, it wouldn't surprise her. After her last salvo, he looked pissed enough to do it one-handed.

But a minute passed and nothing happened. No thud on the door, no sound through the panel. She wiped her nose on her sleeve, made herself look out the window.

In the lamplight, the sleet sheeted down undisturbed.

Cody had taken her at her word. He was gone.

Chapter Eight

AMELIA HAD SAVED the best for last. Brad Ainsley, blind date number three, was definitely the class of the field.

The new history teacher at Amelia's school, he was all of six feet, blond and blue. So blue, in fact, that Julie did a double take to check for colored contacts.

He'd picked the perfect dinner place too, a seafood joint up near Gloucester. They drove up in his hybrid, making the most of a sunny December Sunday, chatting comfortably all the way. They'd both grown up in Newton, graduated the same year from different high schools. He told her about his family, his friends, the master's degree he was working on. He asked about her, seemed interested in her answers, and complimented her hair, her eyes, and her boots.

At a table by the window, overlooking the sea, he ordered clams, she ordered scallops, and they shared like they'd been doing it for years. She laughed at his jokes, he nodded along with her stories, and by the end of the meal they were finishing each other's sentences.

It was nice. It was sweet. It was almost effortless.

And Julie couldn't wait for it to end. Because the whole time, every minute of it, she wished Brad was . . . well, Cody.

It wasn't fair. Brad should be a perfect fit. They liked the same music, the same sports teams, the same food, the same everything. They were practically the same damned person.

But Cody, he was nothing like her. He was from Texas, which might as well be a different country. He was probably a Republican, for God's sake. If they lived together for a hundred years, she'd never be able to finish his sentences.

And then there was the matter of the MD after his name.

Still, she had to admit that when he had his hand up her shirt and his tongue in her mouth, none of that seemed to matter.

Which was why it was a good thing, a *really* good thing, that she'd melted down on him last night. Screeching hysterics, guaranteed to make any sane man run for the hills.

Yes, even though she'd cried herself to sleep, she was glad, really glad, totally glad, that she'd run him off.

It was after eight when Brad pulled onto her street. Fat flurries had begun to fall. Freezing rain was predicted. It would be a dirty night on the roadways.

"Thanks for dinner," she said, hoping he wouldn't ask

to come in. What was the point, with her head all about Cody?

Brad smiled his perfectly nice smile. Dimpleless, but nice all the same. He angled toward her in his seat. "Your sister said you need a date for her wedding." He lilted it into a question at the end.

Ah yes, the wedding. Here was her chance to solve that little problem. Get Amelia off her back, keep her mother from getting involved, and have a perfectly nice time with a guy who, her sister would say, was perfect marriage material.

"Actually, Brad, I already have a date." The not-so-white lie popped out on its own.

His face fell. "Oh. I thought you weren't seeing anyone—"

"It's just a date," she cut in, "nothing serious." And the lies kept on coming. "He's more of a friend, really. And he's gay." She dug herself in deeper.

"You're dating a gay guy?" His blue eyes widened.

"Not dating. He's just coming to the wedding with me." She'd invite Dan. That would redeem her lie, wouldn't it?

Brad touched her arm, all concern. "Whoever he is, Julie, he's not going to switch teams. Gay is gay."

She held up a hand. "Oh, I know that. He's totally gay, no question about it. One hundred percent. And I'm fine with it." How did she get into this?

Brad took her hand, cradled it between his. "Why don't you call him? Tell him you've got a real date."

Why indeed? Why the elaborate charade? Why not take Brad to the wedding and make everyone happy?

He stroked her palm with his fingertips. It should have felt good.

"I can't," she said, "it'll hurt his feelings. He's very sensitive."

For the first time, impatience crept into Brad's voice. "Listen, Julie, I really like you. I want to see you again. I don't understand why you're letting some gay guy get in the way of that." His too-blue-to-be-true eyes burned too intensely.

In the back of her brain, her stalker radar beeped.

"I'm not saying I don't want to see you again." She'd save that news for a phone call. "But the wedding's spoken for."

"Julie." As if repeating her name would bring her into line. Was it some kind of Jedi-mind-control trick? "Let's talk about this inside." He gave her hand a squeeze.

She pulled it away, getting annoyed. "I'm sorry, but the subject's closed." She got out of the car.

He got out too. Came around to her side. Not threatening. Irritating.

"Look, Brad, I'm not backing out on him." It might have started as a lie, but now it was the principle.

"Julie." Again with the name. "He's gay, okay? If he's truly your friend, he'll be glad to step aside for a real man."

Insulted on behalf of "real" gay men everywhere, but vaguely concerned that Brad might be slightly unhinged, she settled for rolling her eyes. Then she set off down the sidewalk. Brad followed behind, repeating her name.

No wonder he was single.

She considered calling Ray to come and chase him off.

But before she could pull out her phone, help rounded the corner in a leather jacket and totally wrong-for-the-weather cowboy boots. Her heart leapt into her throat.

"It's him," she breathed out, meaning the man who'd filled her mind night and day, who she wanted to run to like this was a Nora Ephron film, but she couldn't because she was afraid to move, afraid he was a mirage, because why would he be here except to see her, and why would he want to see her after she was so awful last night?

Hovering behind her, Brad overheard Julie's words and assumed her gay crush had arrived. "I'll take care of this," he said, patting her arm. And throwing back his shoulders, he strode toward Cody, who advanced at his usual crawl.

ALL DAY CODY had fought against it, this near-primal urge to get to Julie. He'd fought it because she was a mess. Wounded and closed up, defensive and hostile. She wanted him, all right; she didn't try to deny it. But she was wrapped too tight to let herself have him.

He'd come close to convincing himself she was too much trouble, hadn't even been sure that when he got here he'd ring her doorbell. But now, seeing her on the sidewalk, red coat swirling, wind whipping her hair, his doubts turned to dust.

She was a train wreck, for sure, but her laughter made him sing. And if he didn't fuck her soon, he might just go crazy.

So yeah, he was in the right place at the right time.

But . . . who was the other guy?

Cody watched him come. Six-foot, good looking. Carried himself like he'd always made the starting lineup. Julie's brother, maybe? Amelia'd said he was coming for the wedding.

The mystery man pulled up and parked in front of Cody, thrust out his hand. "I'm Brad Ainsley. Julie's date."

Her *date*?

He shook the guy's hand, but the testosterone surge made it hard not to crunch his knuckles. "Cody Brown," he bit out. "Julie's friend." He stepped around him, kept walking toward Julie.

Brad fell in beside him. "She told me about you."

"Is that so?" *What did she say?*

"I have to admit, I thought you'd be, you know, more *effeminate*."

Cody pulled up short. *What the fuck?*

He had a couple of inches on ol' Brad and he made the most of them, stepping in till the pretty boy backed up, surprise and a healthy inkling of fear rippling across his prep-school features.

Then Julie popped up between them. Her eyes were jade in the lamplight, and a little amused. Going up on her toes, she dropped a kiss on Cody's cheek, and her lips were so warm on his chilly skin that his testosterone surged in an entirely different direction. His hands closed on her waist, tugging her in.

Her hands went to his shoulders, keeping her distance. Smiling brightly, she said, "I was just telling Brad you're my wedding date."

Excellent. He aimed a king-of-the-jungle smirk at Brad.

Who didn't turn tail like he should have. Instead, he smiled a smugly proprietary smile. "Julie told me you're gay," he said, and Cody's smirk slid sideways. "I respect that," Brad continued, "especially since you're obviously from down South."

Cody saw red. "I'm not from down South, jackass. I'm from *Texas.* And I'm sure as hell not—"

"Cody!" Julie bounced on her toes to get his attention. "Remember what we talked about?"

He turned his glare on her.

"You know," she said, giving him a meaningful look. "About owning your sexual orientation?"

He narrowed his eyes, slid his hands to her hips. "I'm owning it, all right."

"See how good that feels?" She patted him. *Patted* him! Then said, "Just as I was telling Brad how I was going to the wedding with my gay friend, you showed up. Isn't that funny?"

The light dawned. His teeth ground. But he wanted her in his debt, so all he said was, "Har har."

Brad butted in. "I told her you'd be glad to step aside so she could take a real . . . er, date to the wedding. A man with romantic potential."

Yeah, romantic potential. Cody saw through that like glass. The dude was counting on her getting the wedding weepies and throwing herself at the nearest hard body.

Julie locked on Cody. "I told him I don't want to hurt your feelings. I know how sensitive you are."

"That's me. Mr. Sensitive."

She narrowed her eyes. Curled her lip in a snarl only he could see.

He bit back a grin. For some reason, she wanted him to play gay. He didn't know why, but he knew an opportunity when he saw one.

He faked undecided. Chewed his lip. Dragged it out. Then, "I'll have to think about it. Inside. By the fire." *Naked,* he mouthed, out of Brad's sight.

"That's really not necessary," she squeezed out through clenched teeth, "I wouldn't dream of reneging."

He wagged his head. "It's not that simple, Jules. I've got to think of what's best for you. That's why we need to talk it out. Inside. By the fire." *Naked.*

"Heh heh," she managed the phoniest laugh. "You're such a good friend. Honestly, though, I'm good with things as they are."

"But I'm not." His fingers tightened on her hips. "And I'd sure hate to make the *wrong decision* standing out here in the cold. All bundled up in these *clothes.*"

Brad was clueless, but that didn't stop him from getting back in the game. "Listen, Cody. Isn't it obvious what's best for Julie? You're ... well, you're gay, and I'm not." He shrugged, apologetically. "I can give her things you can't."

Cody made a show of sizing him up. "He has a point, Jules—"

"Okay," she blurted, "you're right, we should talk inside." Palms on his chest, she gave him a shove.

He was halfway hard already, but he didn't budge, and

he wouldn't, until the deal was sealed. "You mean by the fire, right?" *Naked.*

Then Brad said to Julie, "I don't see the point of dragging Cody inside with us. What more is there to talk about?"

Could the man really be that dumb?

"Actually," she said, flapping her coat, "Cody and I have some other things to . . . ah, discuss. Personal things."

Her cheeks had gone red, but still Brad hung in. "We were having such a nice time, I thought, well, you know . . ."

Cody took this one. "You thought wrong. Jules doesn't put out on the first date."

Brad backpedaled fast. "I didn't mean—"

"Sure you did." Cody shrugged. "Who could blame you? She's hot." He tugged her against his side. Looped an arm around her shoulders and gave her a squeeze.

She hissed through her teeth, but her body couldn't lie, molding to his like hot wax.

He went the rest of the way hard.

Brad still didn't get it, proving people only see what they want to see. "But the wedding's only two days away," he said. "We need to make plans."

Cody's patience ran out. "Brad, my man, you're kinda dense. So let me break it down for you. Julie's not interested, I'm not gay, and you're not going to the wedding." He smiled, part apology, part triumph, at Brad's offended expression. "Drive safe now, you hear?"

Brad stalked to his car and slammed the door without

another word. Julie called after him. "I had a nice time." Then she whacked Cody's arm. "You didn't have to be mean."

"You didn't have to say I'm gay." He hustled her down the driveway toward the carriage house. "He had to be an idiot to fall for that one."

She snorted. "I hate to break it to you, but in Boston, cowboy boots spell g-a-y."

"Do not."

"Do too."

They made it through the door. He pushed her up against the wall.

"Do not," he mumbled into her throat, opening her coat with both hands.

"Do too," she breathed out, unzipping his jacket, shoving her hands inside.

It was cold in the hallway, but they were on fire. She clawed his shirt up, raked his back with her nails. He arched, pleasure searing through the pain, driving him higher, unleashing animal lust.

He shoved her sweater to her chin, snapped her flimsy bra with one finger. Her breasts, lush and heavy, tumbled into palms, his to handle, his to own. He took her mouth the same way, hot and messy and out of control.

She was wild too, swallowing him up, sucking his tongue like cock. She let out a moan that went straight to his balls, and he lost what was left of his mind. Fighting her zipper, he shoved his hand down her jeans, under soaked satin panties, into liquid heat that sheathed his fingers and drenched his palm. She ground on him, clawing at his belt, tearing at his button flies. When his cock sprang into her hand, that was all it took. No stroking, no nothing, just her fist around him. His vision blurred. Far away, his own voice roared out her name. And he came, long and hard, spilling into her palm, one hand bracing the wall just to keep his feet.

Then she clenched around his fingers, a hot velvet vise that kept him in the game. He pressed deeper, rocked his wrist. Licked her ear, then caught the lobe and bit down. Her breathing went jagged, all hitches and gasps. He heard himself growl, a hungry sound that called for surrender. Everything in her tensed. She vibrated like wire.

And when she let go, sweet Jesus, when she finally released, she shook so hard, then went so limp, he could only pin her to the wall with his chest.

JULIE STRAIGHTENED HER legs, took her own weight on shaky legs.

Cody shifted so his shoulder rolled to the wall. Gently, he extracted his hand from her pants. From her. Then he brought it to his lips, and the humming he made as he sucked his fingers was the sexiest sound she'd ever heard. It ran through her like a shiver.

She met his eyes, half-closed and fixed on her. His cock twitched and she realized she still held it in her hand, slippery and smooth . . . and oh yes, starting to stiffen.

He dropped his hand, the wet one, and covered hers with it, trapping her gaze as he pumped her fist. He brought his lips to her ear. "Time to get naked, darlin'," he breathed, warm and wet. "Time to fuck me."

She swallowed the moan that rose up in her throat. He scraped his teeth over her jaw. Nipped her bottom lip, then pushed his tongue inside, finding hers again, tangling them up.

He was thick and hard now as she stroked her hand up the length of him. There was no resisting it. And why would she want to? If she could get all of him inside her, she wanted every inch.

He pulled away long enough to swing her up into his arms.

"I can walk," she murmured, without conviction.

He crushed her against him. "Save your strength, honey. You're gonna need it."

He all but kicked open the door at the top of the stairs. Crossed the room in three strides and shoved the coffee table aside.

"Fire," he said, going down on his knees. "Naked," as he laid her out on the rug. His hoarse drawl made her girl parts pulse. He'd gone caveman, and she liked it.

She hit the remote and the flame roared to life. Off came her coat. She kicked out of her boots. Started to lift up her sweater, but she glanced over at Cody. And then she forgot to undress.

He sat with his back to her, tugging at his boots. He'd peeled off his T-shirt, exposing a perfect V from shoulders to waist. Sleek muscles rippled under tanned, glossy skin. The maleness of it made her mouth go dry. And the intimacy made her shiver.

His tan line showed at his waist, and she dipped a finger under the edge of elastic. His skin was as taut and smooth as it looked, and even though she'd just held his cock in her hand, it felt like the first time she'd ever touched him.

When he'd stripped completely, he turned to face her. His eyes widened and, slowly, he shook his head no. "Julie, honey, we had a deal."

Going up on his knees, he peeled her sweater over her head, taking her shirt and leaving her bra dangling. Then he sat back on his heels, taking his time. He cocked his head to the side and studied her like a Monet.

"I got a thing for bras," he said at last. "But now I'm thinking that's because I've never seen tits like yours." He reached out, stroked a knuckle along the underside of one breast. Circled the nipple with his thumb, his touch feather-light. She bent her head to watch his big hand caress her, and the sight took her breath.

No man had touched her in three long years. And no man had ever touched her like this.

"No bra tonight," he murmured. He hooked a finger under the strap, drew it over her shoulder. She let it slide from her body.

He took her by the arms, lifted her up on her knees. His fingers stroked over her ribs. His thumbs caught her waistband, tugging her jeans down, over her ass. His cock strained toward her like a compass pointing north. But he was in no hurry.

He was back on Cody time.

Oh so gently, he laid her down. Then he wiggled her jeans off one leg at a time, stroking the backs of her knees, the soles of her feet, making the simple act so erotic that she'd never peel off her jeans again without thinking of this. Of him.

And when he'd stripped her bare, he shifted his body over hers, elbows taking his weight, cock crushed to her thigh, searing her skin.

"Sweetheart," he drawled soft and deep, "I'm about at the end of my rope. You ready for me?"

"I th-think so."

He dropped his chin, nuzzled her neck. "You're soaking wet. I can feel it."

"It's not that." She swallowed. "It's just been a long time. And you're . . . you know."

"Tell me." He rubbed his nose along her jaw. Then lifted his head, kissed the corner of her lips. "Tell me, Jules. What am I?"

He'd probably heard it a hundred times. Why was it so hard to say? "You're bigger than I'm used to."

"You can handle me." He sounded confident. "The tighter, the better."

She must have looked doubtful. He locked onto her eyes. "I'll never hurt you, honey. You're safe with me."

He reached one arm behind him, groped in his jeans and came up with a condom. "Exhibit A." He ripped the packet with his teeth. Rolled it on as she wondered if they came in extra large.

Kneeing her thighs apart, he reached between them, handled her until she forgot to be nervous, until her breath came as rough and ragged as his. When her hips tilted instinctively, he forged in.

Gave her one slow inch at a time.

It wasn't enough. She wanted more, wanted faster. She gave a grunt of impatience. He tsked his tongue. "Always rushing," he chuckled, but the strain made him hoarse. She rolled her head to the side, sank her teeth in his biceps. He dropped his lips to her breast, sucked hard on her nipple.

All of which made things ten thousand times worse.

"Cody, please," she got out.

"Tell me what you want." His voice was thick.

She felt his control fraying. Gave him the words that would snap it. "Please, Cody. Please. *Fuck me hard.*"

"Yes, ma'am," he ground out, and in he drove, grunting when she took him, lifting her hips to give her more. Stroking deep, stroking fast, all the way to the root.

She bucked as he pumped, met each stroke with her own, racing together, frantic and wild. He loomed above her, filling her gaze. She drank in his beauty. Muscle and sinew and bone. Sweat streaked his chest. She smeared her hands through it, raked her nails down his abs. Locked eyes and ate up the hunger she saw.

Then he dropped his chest down on hers. She welcomed his weight. He fisted her hair, panted hard in her ear. "Come with me, baby."

"Yes," she gasped out, snaked a hand in between them.

"Tell me when," he gritted, riding hard, riding fast.

"Now!" She cut loose. "Oh God, now!"

Chapter Nine

CODY FLOPPED ONTO his back, sucking wind like he'd done forty flights at a run. But he couldn't wipe the grin off his face. Thank the sweet baby Jesus he'd swallowed his pride and hunted down Julie. He would have missed the best sex of his life.

He rolled his head to the side. She looked like she'd done the stairs with him, sheened in sweat, cheeks cherry red.

She'd never been prettier.

He rolled up on his side, propped his head on his hand. "The tighter, the better," he said.

She let out a laugh. "I can't disagree."

He traced the line of her jaw. Her eyes were moss green in the firelight. "Told you I wouldn't hurt you."

"Not true. You tortured me with extreme foreplay."

He trailed a finger between her breasts. "Forgot to worry, though, didn't you?"

She tracked her eyes down his chest, all the way to his groin. He followed her gaze, broke into smile. His dick wouldn't scare anyone now.

She smiled too, a sweet curve of her lips that lured him in for a kiss. A gentle kiss this time. Slow and tender. With just a nip at the end to remind her who was boss.

She nipped him right back. The woman never gave him an inch.

He liked that about her.

She snuggled up to him. "I meant it when I told you it's been a long time. Three years. Since David died."

He couldn't imagine going three years—even three months—without getting laid. But he'd never lived with grief like hers.

She reached up a hand, stroked a fingertip along his stubbly jaw. "Thanks for taking the trouble to make it good."

Her tender tone made his throat tighten. "Don't get me wrong, honey, I wanted you to love it. But I can't take much credit, because I was out of my mind most of the time." He captured her hand, brought her palm to his lips. "It was good because we've got something here."

Her eyes had gone soft and mushy. A single tear trembled on her lashes. When it trickled down her temple, his heart rolled over in his chest.

Too moved to speak, he wrapped her up in his arms and rolled onto his back. Her head settled naturally in the notch of his shoulder. She looped her thigh over his, curling around him, and he gathered her in, cupping the curve of her shoulder in one palm, the curve of her bottom in the other.

Sleet slashed at the windows, but it was cozy by the fire. Cody watched the shadows flicker on the walls. Wondered how this woman had gotten so deep under his skin in only four days. Wondered if he was under hers too. If being her first lover in three years meant something, or nothing.

He didn't know how to ask, or even if he wanted to hear the answer. He doubted that one night of hot sex would change her mind about him.

What he needed was time. Time to convince her that not every doctor was all about money. Most of them took up medicine because they wanted to heal people. But it was a hard business, because lots of patients didn't heal. They suffered, and they died, and if you got too attached, took each loss to heart, you'd break into a million pieces.

For sure, some doctors went too far the other way. Their hearts hardened. They got too caught up in the perks. But the truth was, doctors had to detach. It didn't always mean that they didn't care. It meant that they were human.

In time, he could explain all that to Julie. He could make her understand.

But not tonight. For tonight, he wanted her to forget that he was a doctor and see him only as a man.

And as a man, one thing was bugging the shit out of him. He kept his tone casual. "So, what's the deal with Brad?"

She snorted. "Another blind date, courtesy of Amelia."

"She set 'em up for you?"

"Mmm-hmm. She wants me to have a date for her wedding. She threatened to get my mother involved." She shuddered. "Even going on three blind dates is better than that."

"How's it working out for you?" An insouciant drawl.

"Exactly as I expected. Brad was the last of them."

"So . . . all rejects?" He faked a yawn like he wasn't hanging on her answer.

"Yep, every one."

Relief was a lungful of air after sixty seconds under water. He smiled, smugly, and stroked her cheek with his thumb. "You had me going for a minute with the gay thing. I didn't know which one of us you were trying to get rid of, him or me."

She laughed. "Amelia said Brad and I have a lot in common. She was right, he was perfect for me."

His smug smile evaporated. "So what happened?"

"Turns out perfect doesn't do it for me." She snuggled closer. "Besides, I got a stalker-y vibe from him, so it's probably good that he thinks I'm involved with you."

"Are you? Involved with me?"

She slid her hand over his shoulder, played with the ends of his hair. "Do I seem involved?"

It wasn't really an answer.

Then her leg began to move, a slow, deliberate slide that stroked along his cock. Amazingly, he started to stiffen again.

Three erections in an hour—what was he, seventeen?

JULIE SLUMPED FORWARD onto Cody's heaving chest.

"Uh," she grunted out, her own chest heaving. Her thigh muscles sang from the unaccustomed strain. Then he threaded his fingers through her hair, massaging her scalp, and her already gelatinous body went liquid. She couldn't have moved if someone yelled "Fire!"

His hands traveled down from her scalp to her neck. She moaned pathetically. He melted her shoulders, stroked the length of her back . . .

Her own snore startled her awake. She pushed up, wiped her lips with her hand. "Sorry," she said about the drool on his chest. He rubbed it in with his palm. Bodily fluids didn't seem to bother him at all. Good thing, since they were both covered with them.

"I need a shower," she said.

"Sounds good." His hands slid up her thighs. His thumbs met in the middle. "I'm done for now, but you don't have to be." He stroked lightly, but with deadly accuracy. "Tell me you've got one of those removable shower heads."

She nodded, unable to form words.

"I promise you'll never look at it the same way again."

An hour later she was sprawled on her bed, boneless, when Cody strolled out of the bathroom, towel slung around his hips—exactly like her Plaza-lobby vision. Her eyes walked from his feet to his face, taking in the details. Muscled calves. Hipbones sharp enough to hold up the towel. Corrugated abs. Chest carved from marble, arms roped with muscle.

His stubble was dark, his hair finger-combed back. And his eyes, when she met them, were eye-walking her right back. They crinkled as he smiled that outrageous smile.

If she could move, she'd jump him. Again.

His smile widened as if he read her mind. "We need food, Jules. The night's young."

"It is?" she said faintly.

He nodded slowly. "I told you, you gotta keep up your strength."

Oh boy.

He stood her up, pushed her arms into her robe and tied a knot at her waist. Then he prodded her into the kitchen. She opened the fridge, scanned the contents doubtfully. "Steak?"

"Uh-uh." He moved her gently to the other side of the island, sat her on a stool, and went back to the fridge, pulling out eggs and cheese and spinach.

She propped her elbows on the counter, chin in her hands. "I thought men loved steak." David certainly had.

"I don't eat meat," he said.

She sat up straighter. "You're a vegetarian?"

"Mmm-hmm." He broke six eggs into a bowl.

"But . . . you're a guy." All the vegetarians she knew were women. "And you grew up on a ranch."

"Call me a sissy, but I never liked the idea of raising up creatures just to eat 'em."

She watched him whip the eggs. He didn't look like a sissy. Not with the muscles jumping in his forearms. Not with three days' scruff shading his jaw, and that towel slipping lower.

It sagged another inch and she caught a glimpse of something unnaturally white. Leaning over the counter, she gave the towel a tug. It hit the floor, exposing an eight-inch scar as wide as her thumb, slashed diagonally across his left cheek.

"What's that?" She felt personally offended, like she had rights in that cheek.

He looked over his shoulder, followed her gaze. "That," he said, "is the end of my rodeo days."

She goggled. "Seriously? Rodeo?"

"Seriously. Rodeo. Saddle bronc riding."

"Give a Boston girl a hint. What's saddle bronc riding?"

He looked at her like she was a dummy. "Just what it sounds like. You sit in a saddle and hang the hell on while a wild horse tries to pitch you into next week."

Okay, that *was* pretty obvious. "So, were you any good?"

"Hell yeah, I was good! Didn't you see my belt buckle?"

She scratched her head. What did his belt buckle have to do with it?

He picked up his towel, strapped it over his junk before he poured the eggs into the pan. They sizzled and popped. He swirled them around, flexing that forearm again. She practically drooled. A man in the kitchen was hot. Cody in the kitchen was porn. She put him in chaps and a Stetson and her eyes glazed over.

Then he set the omelet in front of her. The scent drifted up her nose.

She could get used to this. She could get used to him.

He took the other stool and half of the omelet, set her straight about the buckle. "In rodeo, the champion gets a belt buckle instead of a trophy."

"So you were a champion saddle bronc rider?" She added a denim shirt and jeans to the Stetson and chaps, had him hold a shiny buckle above his head, displaying it to the cheering crowd.

"Yes, ma'am." He forked in some omelet. "Gearing up for nationals when I landed on a fence while I was training at the ranch. Splintered it, and a big one went deep. I'd have bled out if my brother Tyrell hadn't heard me holler."

"You almost died?" That killed her fantasy. Cody gushing blood made her own blood run cold.

"Like I said, Ty found me in time." He forked in more omelet. "Scared my Mama, though. She put her foot down, shipped me off to college." He shrugged. "I like to compete, so I went back to running."

He pointed his fork at the calendar on the fridge, her running schedule penciled in the large blocks. "Training for the marathon?"

"Mmm-hmm. I've tried before, but it was always half-assed. This time I mean it."

"We could train together." He lilted it into a question.

She met his gaze, let herself steep in his whiskey eyes. For the first time, she noticed an emerald ring around the iris. Was that what made them unique? Because these were no ordinary brown eyes. These, she could look into every day and never get tired of them.

"Um." A question was pending, but she couldn't recall what it was. His eyes crinkled. Oh no. How was she supposed to function under the influence of The Smile?

Then The Smile morphed into The Laugh. She dropped her fork and went for him.

He caught her up in his arms, pulled her onto his lap. His hand was inside her robe before she could untie the knot, her breast in his palm before she could pull his head down to kiss him.

And just like that, they were going at it again. Off came her robe. His towel hit the floor. He swept the plates aside with one arm, sat her up on the counter. "Condom," he got out, and vaulted the sofa to grab his jeans, still crumpled on the floor by the fire.

Then his cell rang.

Oh, he wanted to ignore it; she saw the struggle on his face. But he checked the display, cursed under his breath. And answered it, "This is Dr. Brown."

It hit her like an arctic blast. *Dr.* Brown. That's who he was.

Sliding down from the counter, she pulled on her robe, cold everywhere she'd been hot. Carefully, she scraped the omelets into the trash, then put the plates in the sink and turned the water on hard, trying to drown out the rushing in her ears.

When his arms wrapped around her from behind, she stiffened like a flagpole. He kissed her nape. "Sweetheart, I gotta go. Pileup on the Expressway. They're calling everyone in."

Through frozen lips, she managed to say, "Do you know how to get to the hospital from here?"

"I can find it." He squeezed her lightly, then let her go. She shut off the water, made herself turn around. He was moving faster than she'd ever seen him, scooping up his clothes, hopping one-legged as he stepped into his jeans.

His head popped out through his T-shirt. "I'll be back when I can, okay?"

She put on a plastic smile, strove for casual while she was shaking inside. "Tomorrow's the wedding, so, you know . . ." She let it peter out.

"Yeah, I know. I'm your date, remember?" He smiled, but doubt crept into it.

She flapped a stiff hand, did a phony chuckle. "That was for Brad's benefit. You're not on the hook for the wedding."

He came toward her, unmistakable hurt in his eyes. "Julie. Honey, don't do this." He took her face in his hands, kissed her lips gently. She didn't respond, and when he pulled back to meet her eyes, she looked down.

"Be careful," she said. "It's slippery outside."

He let his hands fall. "I'll be back as soon as I can," he repeated. Then he took his jacket and went out. She heard his boots pound the stairs, the door thump below. And all was still.

She stood rooted in place as the sleet lashed the windows. Then a shiver ran through her from her head to her toes. She clasped her robe, but the cold came from within, wrapping around her throat, freezing her lips.

As her body chilled, her mind overheated. Her thoughts jumbled together, a montage of despair. Cody sprinting through the cold. Victims bleeding on the pavement. David sucking his last breath. The grisly images ran together, indelibly linked, engraved on her brain.

Like a fast-moving poison, panic spread through her veins. She clutched the counter like it was her sanity, watched her knuckles turn white with the strain. *This* was why she steered clear of doctors. They stirred up the past, stuck a knife in her pain.

She'd been doing just fine before Cody came along with his drawl and his smile. She'd made a mistake letting him get close, and she was paying for it now with angst and cold sweat.

But it was over, she was done with him. Tomorrow, she'd dish him off on Murph, send a text to let him know.

And even if it meant moving out of Beacon Hill, she'd make sure she never saw Cody Brown again.

Chapter Ten

"DR. BROWN." A hand shook his shoulder. He rolled away from it, burrowing into the pillow. "Cody." A harder shake. "Go home."

Those last words got his attention. He forced his eyes open, scrubbed his hands over his face. "What time is it?" The words crunched like ground glass in his dry throat.

"Almost noon."

"Shit." He swung his legs off the spare bed he'd crashed out on, worked up a half smile for Marianne and glugged the sludgy coffee she handed him. "You missed a hell of a night."

"So I hear. It's turned to snow, but there's still ice underneath, so be careful out there." She eyed his boots. "Better switch to L.L.Bean for the winter." She laughed when he shuddered. "Have you hooked up with Julie Marone yet?"

He shrugged into his jacket. "Going to see her right now."

Marianne looked surprised. "I know she's dedicated, but showing condos on Christmas Eve?" She shrugged a shoulder. "Well, I suppose you're in a hurry to get Betsy out here."

"You bet." Everyone at the hospital assumed Betsy was his girl. He'd never corrected them. It was simpler that way, at least for now.

Outside, snow fell in a white sheet. The pavement around the hospital had been plowed and treated, the main roads too, so footing wasn't a problem there.

But when he crossed Charles Street and began the climb up into Beacon Hill, his boots might as well have been greased. "Fuck!" he yelled, skating backward toward the roadway.

By sheer luck, he snagged a light pole with one hand. Momentum wound him around it until he hugged it like a lover. Grateful to be alive, he dredged up a rusty prayer of thanks as the cars *shissed* past an arm's length away.

He'd caught his breath and was considering his options, all of them embarrassing, when an off-duty cab pulled up alongside him. The cabbie lowered the window, looked him over. "Not from around here, are you, pal?"

Cody scratched his head like he was puzzled. "Can't figure out why folks keep asking me that," he drawled.

The guy chuckled. "Get in, cowboy."

Letting go of the pole, Cody slid sideways till his hip bumped the door, then sighed profoundly when his ass hit the duct-taped seat.

The cabbie eyed him in the mirror. "Place a couple blocks up. Outdoor gear. Boots, gloves. That kinda shit."

"Appreciate it," Cody said, hoping Julie would appreciate the lengths he was going to get back to her. She'd been upset when he left, but in his experience, women often got upset when he ran out in the middle of sex. Most of the time, they were over it when he got back, and happy to pick up where they left off.

An hour later, tricked out for a moonwalk, he leaned on her bell and waited for her to come downstairs and make fun of him.

But she didn't come. He rang again. Then once more.

He snooped around, spotted footprints mostly covered with fresh snow. Maybe she'd gone to the store. Yeah. He could meet up with her, carry the groceries.

Sheltering under the tiny overhang, he punched her number into his phone. It rang and rang, finally went to voicemail.

He slumped against the door, stared out at the falling snow. And made himself consider that maybe—and he could hardly believe it—but maybe, after all that hot sex and cuddling and staring into each other's eyes, she was blowing him off.

Or maybe not. Maybe she'd gone off to Amelia's to do wedding stuff. Maybe she just forgot to leave him a note or a text or a voicemail to let him know.

It could happen.

He clomped off in that direction, cursing the storm that had dragged him out of her arms.

Ray answered the door in sock feet. "Hey, Cody. Come on in."

Cody stomped off the snow and stepped into the hallway. He shook Ray's hand. "Today's the day. You ready?"

"I guess." Ray checked his watch. "Four more hours as a bachelor." He grinned. "Want a beer?"

Cody shook his head with regret. "It'd knock me on my ass." He glanced over Ray's shoulder. "Julie here?"

"She's off with Amelia, doing stuff at the church. They're getting dressed there too, so they won't be back."

"Where's the church?"

Ray looked down at his socks. "I'm not supposed to tell you."

Cody's jaw dropped. "What the fuck?"

"Sorry." Ray rubbed his toe on the tile. "Jules was pretty strong about it. Amelia tried to change her mind, but . . ." He shrugged.

Cody scratched his jaw. Three days growth, and counting. "I could beat it out of you."

Ray's eyes bugged. "Shit, Cody, you'd break me in half!"

"Yep. So why don't we just cut to the chase? Tell 'em I roughed you up and you spilled your guts."

Ray considered it. "Wouldn't that leave, you know, bruises?"

"Say I went Jack Bauer on you. No marks, just pain."

Ray perked up. "Remember that time he was gonna pop a guy's eye out with a pen? Let's say that."

"You got it." Cody nodded along. "Now where's the fucking church?"

THE CHURCH WAS small, more of a chapel. Grey stone walls, worn wooden pews. Statues in each corner of Jesus and Mary, Joseph and St. Francis. Votives flickered in red glass at their feet.

Amelia surveyed the modest altar, bordered with a double tier of red and white poinsettias. "A Christmas Eve wedding sure saves a bundle on flowers," she observed.

"Mmm." Julie didn't look up. She looped a white bow over the end of a pew. Moved on to the next one.

"More money for heroin and hookers on the honeymoon," Amelia went on.

"Mmm."

"Less to regret during the inevitable divorce."

"Uh-huh."

Amelia walked up behind her, poked her in the side.

"AHHHHH!" Julie leapt four feet. "What the hell, Amelia!"

"Just making sure you weren't replaced by a robot."

Julie glared. "Very funny."

"Seriously. It's my *wedding day* and you're not even *into* it."

Julie had to give her that one. "Sorry. I'll do better." She grinned an extra-toothy grin.

Amelia rolled her eyes, relieved her of some of the ribbons. "You can make it up to me by telling me who you're bringing to the wedding. I don't know why it's such a big secret."

Julie plunked down in a pew, came out with the truth she'd been ducking all day. "Listen sweetie, I hate to disappoint you on your wedding day, but I'm not bringing a date."

Amelia threw up a hand. "Not even Brad? For God's sake, Jules, he's perfect!"

Julie weighed her words. "He seems very nice. Good looking. Easy to talk to."

"So what's the problem?"

"He just . . . didn't do it for me."

Amelia put her hand on her hip. "Admit it. You want Cody."

"No, I don't." Julie said it too quickly, felt heat creep up her neck. She turned her back on her sister and fiddled with the ribbons.

But Amelia wouldn't drop it. "What if he wasn't a doctor? What then?"

"It doesn't matter. He *is* a doctor."

"Jules—"

"It's a deal breaker," Julie cut in, "and it's not negotiable."

"But—"

"Enough!" Julie chopped a hand through the air. The long night dragged at her, both the good parts and the bad, fraying her patience, shredding her nerves. "You don't understand, Amelia. You weren't there at the hospital, in the doctor's offices, the waiting rooms."

She slapped the ribbons down on a pew. "You didn't smell the horrible smells. Medicine and antiseptic and vomit and shit. You didn't see the hope live and die in David's eyes every time some doctor offered him a lifeline that broke as soon as he grabbed it."

Anger boiled over into tears. They spilled down her

cheeks. It was the worst time for a breakdown, but she couldn't stop.

"The doctors," she raved, "they walked in and out of our lives like . . . like waiters or doormen or the salesclerk at Store 24. We were just customers to them. They showed up for ten minutes and they got paid, live or die. They didn't even care which it was!"

She was sobbing now, overtired and babbling, making no sense because her thoughts no longer made sense, even to her. "Don't you see? The doctors, they're all about suffering, and dying, and playing golf at their country clubs. They can't really do anything, they just want people to think they can so they can take their money and leave them with nothing. *Nothing.*"

Amelia had her by the shoulders. She pulled her into a hug, stroked her hair. "Oh honey, I'm so sorry."

Julie shook in her arms, throat hitching, nose streaming. "Cody reminds me," she got out. "He reminds me how it was. I can't go there again. I can't do it."

"It's okay, baby," her sister crooned. "You don't have to see him. You don't have to see Cody ever again."

"Like hell she doesn't," boomed a voice from the back of the church. "I'm damned if I'll take the heat for every fucked-up doctor and incurable cancer in the whole fucking world."

Cody strode down the aisle, long legs eating up the distance at ten times his normal pace. Snow fell in clumps from his shoulders, flew off the hood he shoved back. His eyes burned, his teeth showed, and the set of his hard, scruffy jaw said he was madder than hell.

Watching him come, Julie didn't know what to do. Fear and desire and guilt and grief all did battle in her head and her heart. Unable to choose between fight or flight, she froze like a rabbit, while Amelia, brave Amelia, stepped in front of her.

"Cody—"

"You should go to Ray," he said. "I had to beat the church out of him."

Amelia's mouth formed an O. Her fists balled at her sides. "Ray's half your size! If you hurt him . . . If you hurt my sister . . ."

"I've never hurt a woman and I'm not starting in church on Christmas Eve. Now go help your man before it's too late."

"Jules, come with me." She gripped Julie's arm.

"Just go," Julie said, knowing it was a ploy. Cody'd never hurt Ray. What he might do to her, she didn't know, but any pain he inflicted wouldn't be physical.

She faced off with him as Amelia fled. "Have your say, tough guy," she said, finding her nerve. "And then go away. You're not invited to this wedding."

He advanced on her till he was glowering down. She held her ground, wiped her nose on her sleeve. Nothing like having it out without a tissue in sight.

"You ran out on me," he growled, a menacing drawl. "I went through hell and high water to get back to you, and you ran out on me."

"Funny, I remember *you* leaving *me*."

"People were hurt. They needed me. I got home as soon as I could."

He didn't notice that he'd called her place home, but she did. It made her want to reach out and hold him.

She dug in her heels. "Listen, Cody." Her voice lacked force. She bucked it up. "You're a nice guy—"

"No I'm not." He leaned in. "I'm all kinds of trouble. And I won't walk away and make this easy. You're a mess, Jules, a fucked-up head case."

She flinched like he'd slapped her. His lip curled up. "I told you I wasn't nice. But I *am* honest. Which you're not. You want to blame all the shit in the world on the men in white coats, even though you know it's bullshit."

His words stung, but she fell back on her usual retort. "You don't understand—"

"The hell I don't. I just stood over a twelve-year-old girl who won't see Christmas this year. I had to tell her mother, who punched me right here with her fist." He slapped his chest. "You want to hit me, Jules? Will that make you feel better?" He spread his arms. "Take your shot. It won't change a thing."

She shook her head, backed away. Nothing made sense when he was near.

He lowered his arms, took a deep breath. When he spoke again, his voice was gentle.

"I know you want to blame somebody. You want to find a reason for the whole shitty thing. I can't help you with that. I can't tell you why David died, or why anyone dies. Most of the time, it seems pretty random. But I can tell you this. *Another* twelve-year-old girl is alive right now because I went to the hospital last night. I saved her life. *Her* mother didn't lose a daughter."

Julie hung her head, shame and sorrow crowding out anger, leaving her more confused than ever. Silent tears streamed, but for once they weren't bubbling with rage.

Cody raised her chin with two fingers. Tilted his head to one side. "Tell me Jules, are you really gonna hold that against me?"

Was she? Was she going to carry her grudge past the point of all reason? Use it as a sword to wound herself? To wound Cody? Or could she lay it down, right here, on Christmas Eve, and begin again? The only thing stopping her was herself. All she had to do was let go.

Taking a deep breath, she sighed it out, then let her fists unclench. It was hard to do. She'd clutched David's pain so tight for so long, but now it seemed to lift from her palms, impatient to take flight, freeing her hands to hold on to someone else. *At last.*

She gave Cody a watery smile. "Well, when you put it that way," she said.

He hauled her against him, wrapped her up in his arms. She let herself love it, buried her face in his warm, solid chest as he rocked her. When she snuffled, he murmured, "Go ahead, honey, wipe your nose on my shirt." She did, and then she laughed.

"That's one good thing about doctors," she said. "Nothing grosses you out, even snot."

JULIE'S UNCLE ARTURO hosted the reception for twenty in the back room of his North End restaurant. Her cousin Jan—his daughter—cornered her at the bar.

"Dr. Delicious really fills out that suit," Jan said slyly, then cut a sloe-eyed glance at Cody, heading their way.

Julie stuck her pinky in her ear, jiggled it like she was hearing things.

Jan giggled. "What can I say? Dr. Do-Me-Against-The-Wall brings out my inner slut."

Julie slewed a glance around to make sure Uncle Arturo didn't hear. "Where did you learn to talk like that?"

Jan rolled her eyes. "Where do you think I learned it, *Julie*? I'm trying to be more like you. Confident. Professional. Totally together."

"Jan, I've never said any such thing—" Then she lost her train of thought as Cody's big hand settled on the small of her back. His heat soaked through the filmy silk of her dress.

He smiled at Jan, effectively tying her tongue. She tottered off, her inner vixen no match for the likes of Cody Brown.

Before Julie could scold him, he stroked his thumb along her spine. Just a couple of inches, up and down, but she felt the tingle all the way up to her scalp and all the way down to her bottom.

"Nice party," he said, "great food, good wine. Can we go home now?"

There, he did it again. Called her place home.

He leaned down to take a bite out of her ear, his breath hot against her throat. "If you recall," he whispered, "I didn't get any sleep last night, what with banging you six ways to Sunday." His hand slid lower, his fingers just touching the curve of her ass. "Let's go home and I'll bang you some more."

Again with the home. It felt totally right. So did the part about banging her.

She nodded and he made tracks for the coatroom. The bride and groom had already departed for St. John, so they breezed through their goodbyes and hit the sidewalk in three minutes flat, snagging one of the cabs Uncle Arturo had lined up at the curb.

As they rode through the snow, Cody took her hand and pulled it onto his lap, lacing their fingers. Her stomach jittered with both anticipation and nerves. Cody had brought her back to life, body, and soul, just as if she'd woken up on a warm, sunny beach after hibernating through a cold, hard winter. But she was scared too, because she had no idea where this was going.

She knew what she wanted. The fairy tale. The happy ending. And for the first time since David died, she believed that maybe she'd get it someday.

But this thing with Cody was so new. So not what she expected. She *thought* she was over the doctor thing, but *was* she?

And then, out of the blue, in a crisp Kodak moment, she saw it. Red brick, green shutters, halfway up Mount Vernon Street, with a tiny yard out back for Betsy.

Their dream house.

Cody must have heard her gasp, because he caught her chin with one finger, turned her face to his. "What's up? You okay?"

She looked into his warm whiskey eyes. They were

filled with concern for her, and affection. She squeezed his hand. "You like Beacon Hill, don't you?"

"Love it."

"Great. Because I just figured out the perfect place for you."

"Okaaay," he said, "but there's no rush, is there?" He dropped his eyes to their hands, rubbed her knuckle with his thumb. "I kinda like your place." He sounded shy. "*You're* there."

Oh my. Her heart did a tipsy pirouette in her chest. Then, without stopping to wonder whether it was wise, it tumbled happily downhill and fell in love.

It stunned her, the sudden completeness of it. For one breathless moment she paused to enjoy it. Then, squeezing his hand, she brought it to her lips for a kiss. He looked up in surprise, and she smiled.

"I promise you, Cody," she said with conviction, "this house will have everything you want in a home."

Trust me. It'll even have me.

If you liked Cody, then you'll love his brother Tyrell in

THE WEDDING FAVOR

the first full-length novel in the Save the Date *series by Avon Books rising star*

CARA CONNELLY!

Available in print and ebook in January 2014!

***

IN HER DELICIOUSLY sexy debut novel, Cara Connelly gives a whole new meaning to *crashing a wedding* . . .

Before the Wedding

TYRELL BROWN WANTED to get the hell out of Houston and back to his ranch. Instead, he's stuck on a flight to France for his best friend's wedding. To top it off, he discovers he's sharing a seat with Victoria Westin, the blue-eyed, stiletto-heeled lawyer who's been a thorn in his side for months.

At the Wedding

VICTORIA CAN'T BELIEVE it! How can she be at the same wedding as this long, lean cowboy with a killer smile? So what if they shared a few in-flight cocktails, some serious flirting, and a near-miss at the mile-high club? She still can't stand the man!

After the Wedding

THE WEDDING DISASTER's in the rearview, but the sizzle between these two is still red-hot. They tried to be on their best behavior in France, but back in the states, all bets are off . . .

Continue reading for a sneak peek at

THE WEDDING FAVOR

An Excerpt from

THE WEDDING FAVOR

"THAT WOMAN"—TYRELL aimed his finger like a gun at the blonde across the hall—"is a bitch on wheels."

Angela set a calming hand on his arm. "That's why she's here, Ty. That's why they sent her."

He paced away from Angela, then back again, eyes locked on the object of his fury. She was talking on a cell phone, angled away from him so all he could see was her smooth French twist and the simple gold hoop in her right earlobe.

"She's got ice water in her veins," he muttered. "Or arsenic. Or whatever the hell they embalm people with."

"She's just doing her job. And in this case, it's a thankless one. They can't win."

Ty turned his roiling eyes on Angela. He would have started in—again—about hired-gun lawyers from New York City coming down to Texas thinking all they had to do was bullshit a bunch of good ole boys who'd never made it past eighth grade, but just then the clerk stepped out of the judge's chambers.

"Ms. Sanchez," she said to Angela. "Ms. Westin," to the blonde. "We have a verdict."

Across the hall, the blonde snapped her phone shut and dropped it into her purse, snatched her briefcase off the tile floor, and without looking at Angela or Ty, or anyone else, for that matter, walked briskly through the massive oak doors and into the courtroom. Ty followed several paces behind, staring bullets in the back of her tailored navy suit.

Twenty minutes later they walked out again. A reporter from *Houston Tonight* stuck a microphone in Ty's face.

"The jury obviously believed you, Mr. Brown. Do you feel vindicated?"

I feel homicidal, he wanted to snarl. But the camera was rolling. "I'm just glad it's over," he said. "Jason Taylor dragged this out for seven years, trying to wear me down. He didn't."

He continued striding down the broad hallway, the reporter jogging alongside.

"Mr. Brown, the jury came back with every penny of the damages you asked for. What do you think that means?"

"It means they understood that all the money in the world won't raise the dead. But it can cause the living some serious pain."

"Taylor's due to be released next week. How do you feel knowing he'll be walking around a free man?"

Ty stopped abruptly. "While my wife's cold in the

ground? How do you think I feel?" The man shrank back from Ty's hard stare, decided not to follow as Ty strode out through the courthouse doors.

Outside, Houston's rush hour was a glimpse inside the doors of hell. Scorching pavement, blaring horns. Eternal gridlock.

Ty didn't notice any of it. Angela caught up to him on the sidewalk, tugged his arm to slow him down. "Ty, I can't keep up in these heels."

"Sorry." He slowed to half speed. Even as pissed off as he was, Texas courtesy was ingrained.

Taking her bulging briefcase from her hand, he smiled down at her in a good imitation of his usual laid-back style. "Angie, honey," he drawled, "you could separate your shoulder lugging this thing around. And believe me, a separated shoulder's no joke."

"I'm sure you'd know about that." She slanted a look up from under thick black lashes, swept it over his own solid shoulders. Angling her slender body toward his, she tossed her wavy black hair and tightened her grip on his arm.

Ty got the message. The old breast-crushed-against-the-arm was just about the easiest signal to read.

And it came as no surprise. During their long days together preparing for trial, the cozy take-out dinners in her office as they went over his testimony, Angela had dropped plenty of hints. Given their circumstances, he hadn't encouraged her. But she was a beauty, and to be honest, he hadn't discouraged her either.

Now, high on adrenaline from a whopping verdict

that would likely boost her to partner, she had "available" written all over her. At that very moment they were passing by the Alden Hotel. One nudge in that direction and she'd race him to the door. Five minutes later he'd be balls deep, blotting out the memories he'd relived on the witness stand that morning. Memories of Lissa torn and broken, pleading with him to let her go, let her die. Let her leave him behind to somehow keep living without her.

Angela's steps slowed. He was tempted, sorely tempted.

But he couldn't do it. For six months Angela had been his rock. It would be shameful and ugly to use her this afternoon, then drop her tonight.

Because drop her, he would. She'd seen too deep inside, and like the legions preceding her, she'd found the hurt there and was all geared up to fix it. He couldn't be fixed. He didn't want to be fixed. He just wanted to fuck and forget. And she wasn't the girl for that.

Fortunately, he had the perfect excuse to ditch her.

"Angie, honey." His drawl was deep and rich even when he wasn't using it to soften a blow. Now it flowed like molasses. "I can't ever thank you enough for all you did for me. You're the best lawyer in Houston and I'm gonna take out a full-page ad in the paper to say so."

She leaned into him. "We make a good team, Ty." Sultry-eyed, she tipped her head toward the Marriott. "Let's go inside. You can . . . buy me a drink."

His voice dripped with regret, not all of it feigned. "I wish I could, sugar. But I've got a plane to catch."

She stopped on a dime. "A *plane*? Where're you going?"

"Paris. I've got a wedding."

"But Paris is just a puddle-jump from here! Can't you go tomorrow?"

"France, honey. Paris, France." He flicked a glance at the revolving clock on the corner, then looked down into her eyes. "My flight's at eight, so I gotta get. Let me find you a cab."

Dropping his arm, she tossed her hair again, defiant this time. "Don't bother. My car's back at the courthouse." Snatching her briefcase from him, she checked her watch. "Gotta run, I have a date." She turned to go.

And then her bravado failed her. Looking over her shoulder, she smiled uncertainly. "Maybe we can celebrate when you get back?"

Ty smiled too, because it was easier. "I'll call you."

Guilt pricked him for leaving the wrong impression, but Jesus, he was itching to get away from her, from everyone, and lick his wounds. And he really did have a plane to catch.

Figuring it would be faster than finding a rush-hour cab, he walked the six blocks to his building, working up the kind of sweat a man only gets wearing a suit. He ignored the elevator, loped up the five flights of stairs—why not, he was soaked anyway—unlocked his apartment, and thanked God out loud when he hit the air-conditioning.

The apartment wasn't home—that would be his ranch—just a sublet, a place to crash during the run-up to the trial. Sparsely furnished and painted a dreary off-white, it had suited his bleak and brooding mood.

And it had one appliance he was looking forward

to using right away. Striding straight to the kitchen, he peeled off the suit parts he was still wearing—shirt, pants, socks—and balled them up with the jacket and tie. Then he stuffed the whole wad in the trash compactor and switched it on, the first satisfaction he'd had all day.

The clock on the stove said he was running late, but he couldn't face fourteen hours on a plane without a shower, so he took one anyway. And of course he hadn't packed yet.

He hated to rush, it went against his nature, but he moved faster than he usually did. Even so, what with the traffic, by the time he parked his truck and went through all the rigmarole to get to his terminal, the plane had already boarded and they were preparing to detach the Jetway.

Though he was in no frame of mind for it, he forced himself to dazzle and cajole the pretty girl at the gate into letting him pass, then settled back into his black mood as he walked down the Jetway. Well, at least he wouldn't be squished into coach with his knees up his nose all the way to Paris. He'd sprung for first class and he intended to make the most of it. Starting with a double shot of Jack Daniel's.

"Tyrell Brown, can't you move any faster than that? I got a planeful of people waiting on you."

Despite his misery, he broke out in a grin at the silver-haired woman glaring at him from the airplane door. "Loretta, honey, you working this flight? How'd I get so lucky?"

She rolled her eyes. "Spare me the sweet talk and move

your ass." She waved away the ticket he held out. "I don't need that. There's only one seat left on the whole dang airplane. Why it has to be in my section, I'll be asking the good Lord next Sunday."

He dropped a kiss on her cheek. She swatted his arm. "Don't make me tell your mama on you." She gave him a little shove down the aisle. "I talked to her just last week and she said you haven't called her in a month. What kind of ungrateful boy are you, anyway? After she gave you the best years of her life."

Loretta was his mama's best friend, and she was like family. She'd been needling him since he was a toddler, and was one of the few people immune to his charm. She pointed at the only empty seat. "Sit your butt down and buckle up so we can get this bird in the air."

Ty had reserved the window seat, but it was already taken, leaving him the aisle. He might have objected if the occupant hadn't been a woman. But again, Texas courtesy required him to suck it up, so he did, keeping one eye on her as he stuffed his bag in the overhead.

She was leaning forward, rummaging in the carry-on between her feet, and hadn't seen him yet, which gave him a chance to check her out.

Dressed for travel in a sleek black tank top and yoga pants, she was slender, about five-foot-six, a hundred and twenty pounds, if he was any judge. Her arms and shoulders were tanned and toned as an athlete's, and her long blond hair was perfectly straight, falling forward like a curtain around a face that he was starting to hope lived up to the rest of her.

Things are looking up, he thought. *Maybe this won't be one of the worst days of my life after all.*

Then she looked up at him. The bitch on wheels.

He took it like a fist in the face, spun on his heel, and ran smack into Loretta.

"For God's sake, Ty, what's wrong with you!"

"I need a different seat."

"Why?"

"Who cares why. I just do." He slewed a look around the first-class cabin. "Switch me with somebody."

She set her fists on her hips, and in a low but deadly voice, said, "No, I will not switch you. These folks are all in pairs and they're settled in, looking forward to their dinner and a good night's sleep, which is why they're paying through the nose for first class. I'm not asking them to move. And neither are you."

It *would* be Loretta, the only person on earth he couldn't sweet-talk. "Then switch me with someone from coach."

Now she crossed her arms. "You don't want me to do that."

"Yes I do."

"No you don't and I'll tell you why. Because it's a weird request. And when a passenger makes a weird request, I'm obliged to report it to the captain. The captain's obliged to report it to the tower. The tower notifies the marshals, and next thing you know, you're bent over with a finger up your butt checking for C-4." She cocked her head to one side. "Now, do you really want that?"

He really didn't. "Sheeee-iiiit," he squeezed out between his teeth. He looked over his shoulder at the bitch on wheels. She had her nose in a book, ignoring him.

Fourteen hours was a long time to sit next to someone you wanted to strangle. But it was that or get off the plane, and he couldn't miss the wedding.

He cast a last bitter look at Loretta. "I want a Jack Daniel's every fifteen minutes till I pass out. You keep 'em coming, you hear?"

Be sure to watch for

THE WEDDING VOW

the second novel in the Save the Date *series by*

CARA CONNELLY!

Available from Avon Impulse in Fall 2014!

FIVE YEARS AGO, as a bloodthirsty young prosecutor, Madeline St. Clair damn near took down Adam LeCroix for lifting a Renoir out from under half a dozen armed guards. That's a brush with justice that the billionaire playboy can't forgive or forget.

Now the shoe is on the other foot. Adam's favorite—and legally acquired—Monet has been heisted from his Portofino mansion, and the insurance company, citing his questionable past, refuses to pay up. So Adam hunts down Maddie, now an associate at a high-dollar law firm, and gives her an ultimatum—work for him against the insurance company, or he'll use his influence to make sure she doesn't work at all.

Maddie would rather chew glass than work for Adam, but as he draws her deeper into his life, Maddie learns there's a heart hiding under the sexy villain's hard-ass veneer. Is there a chance the law-and-order lawyer and the fast-and-loose felon can put the past behind them and write their own wedding vow?

Read on for a sneak peek at

THE WEDDING VOW

An Excerpt from

THE WEDDING VOW

SIX THOUSAND EIGHT hundred dollars and ninety-eight cents.

Maddie let the bill flutter to her desk, where it settled like a leaf between her elbows. She dropped her head into her hands.

Lucille, her lovable, irresponsible, artistic sister, wanted to do a semester in Italy, studying the great masters.

Well, hell, who wouldn't? The problem was, Lucy's private college tuition was already stretching Maddie to the max. The extra expense of a semester abroad meant dipping into—no, wiping out—her meager emergency fund.

Still, considering all they'd been through, Lucy's carefree spirit was nothing short of a miracle. If keeping that miracle alive meant slaving more hours at her desk, Maddie would make it work somehow.

Knuckles rapped sharply on her office door—Adrianna Marchand's signature staccato. Maddie slid a file on top of the bill as Adrianna strode in.

"Madeline. South conference room. Now." Adrianna scraped an eye over Maddie's hair and makeup, her sleeveless blouse. "Full armor."

Maddie shook her head. "Take Randall. I'm due in court in two hours and I'm still not up to speed on this case." Insurance defense might be the most boring legal work in the world, but it was also complex, and she was buried. She waved an arm at the boxes stacked on her cherry coffee table, the hundred case files that marched the length of her leather sofa. "Remember how you dumped all of Vicky's cases on me after you *fired her for no reason?*"

Adrianna iced over. "*No one's* job is guaranteed at this firm."

Maddie glared, unwilling to show fear. But she was outclassed and she knew it. Adrianna's stare could freeze the fires of hell, and as one of Marchand, Riley, and White's founding partners, she could, and would, fire Maddie's ass if she pushed back too hard.

"Fine, whatever." Kicking off her fuzzy slippers and shoving her feet into the red Jimmy Choos she kept under her desk, Maddie whipped the jacket of her black silk Armani suit off the back of her chair and punched her fists through the sleeves. Then she spread her arms. "Full armor. Satisfied?"

"Touch up your makeup."

Rolling her eyes, Maddie dug a compact out of her

purse, brushed some color onto her pale cheeks, hit her lips with some gloss. Then she poked her fingers into her caramel hair to give it some lift. She wore it spiked, like her heels, to make herself look taller, but at a petite five feet she was still a shrimp.

Adrianna nodded once, then charged out the door, setting a brisk pace down the carpeted hallway. "Step on it. We've kept your new client waiting too long."

Maddie had to trot to keep up. "*My* new client? Because I don't have enough work?"

"He requested you specifically. He says you're acquainted."

"Well, who is he?"

"He wants to surprise you." Adrianna's dry tone made it clear she wasn't kidding.

Before Maddie could respond to that ridiculous statement, Adrianna tapped politely on the conference room door, then gently pushed it open.

Meant for large meetings with important clients, the room was designed to impress, with Oriental carpets covering the hardwoods, and original landscapes by notable artists gracing the walls. But it was the long cherry table that really set the tone. Polished to a gleam and surrounded by posh leather chairs, it spelled confidence, professionalism, and prosperity.

Bring us your problem, that table said, *and we will solve it without breaking a sweat.*

And if the room and the table weren't enough to convince a prospective client that Marchand, Riley, and White were all that, then the million-dollar view of the

Manhattan skyline through the forty-foot-wide glass wall would drive the point home. Who could argue with that kind of success?

Now Maddie's new client stood gazing out at that view, his back to the door, one hand in the pocket of his expensively cut trousers, the other holding a sleek cell phone to his ear.

Through that phone, Maddie heard a woman's tinkling laughter. He responded in rapid Italian. Not that Maddie understood a word of it. Her Italian began and ended with ordering risotto in Little Italy. But she'd had a short fling with a gorgeous Italian waiter, and she recognized the rhythm of the language. It was the sound of sweaty sex.

Clearing her throat to announce their presence earned her a wintry glance from Adrianna. But the man ignored them utterly. Maddie crossed her arms and looked him up and down with an affronted eye.

He was tall, over six feet, and she put his weight at a lean one-ninety. Broad through the shoulders, narrow at the hips, he bore himself like an athlete, graceful and relaxed—as if he wasn't standing six scant inches from thin air, sixty stories above Fifth Avenue.

Though he claimed to know her, she couldn't place him by the sliver of his face reflected in the glass, or by the sleek, black hair curling over his collar, too long for Wall Street, not long enough for the Italian soccer team.

Everything about him—his clothes, his bearing, his flagrant arrogance—screamed rich, confident, and entitled.

He must be mistaken about her, she decided, because she honestly didn't know anyone like him. And given his casual assumption that his time was more important than theirs, she didn't want to.

She held it together for as long as she could, tapping her foot, biting her tongue, but as the grandfather clock in the corner ticked into the fifth long minute of silent subservience, her patience ran out. She uncrossed her arms and reached for the doorknob. "I don't have time for this shit."

Adrianna's hand shot out and clamped her arm. "Suck it up, Madeline," she gritted through her teeth.

"Why should I? Why should *you*?" Under normal circumstances, Adrianna had zero tolerance for disrespect, so why was she putting up with this guy's bullshit?

Flinging a resentful look at the mystery man, she didn't bother to lower her voice. "This guy doesn't know me. Because seriously, if he did, he'd know I won't stand here burning daylight while he talks dirty to his girlfriend."

"Oh yes you will," Adrianna hissed. She released Maddie's arm, but caught her eyes. "You'll stand on your head if he says so. He could mean *millions* for this firm."

The man in question chose that moment to end his call. Casually, unhurriedly, he slipped the phone in his pocket. Then he turned to face them.

Maddie's heart stopped. Her lips went icy.

Adrianna started to speak but he cut her off, his vaguely European accent smoothing the edge from his words. "Thank you, Adrianna. Now give us the room."

Without a word, Adrianna nodded once and left them alone, closing the door softly behind her.

His complete attention came to rest on Maddie, a laser beam disguised as cool condescension. Her blood, which had gone cold, now boiled up in response, pounding her temples, hammering out a beat called Unresolved Fury, Frustrated Objectives, Justice Denied.

"You son of a bitch," she snarled. "How dare you claim an acquaintance with me?"

He smiled, a deceptively charming curve of the lips meant to distract the unwary from eyes so intensely blue and so penetratingly sharp that they might otherwise reveal him as the diabolical felon he was.

"Ms. St. Clair." Her name sounded faintly exotic on his tongue. "Surely you don't deny that we know each other."

"Oh, I know you, Adam LeCroix. I know you should be doing ten to fifteen in Leavenworth."

His lips curved another half inch, past charming, to amused. "And I know you. I know that if you'd taken me to trial, you'd have done an excellent job of it. But"—he shrugged slightly—"both of us know that no jury would have convicted me."

"Still so cocky," she simmered. "And so fucking guilty."

ADAM HELD BACK a laugh. Madeline St. Clair might be tiny enough to fit in his pocket, but she had the grit of a two-hundred-pound cage fighter.

When he'd last seen her five years ago, she was a bloodthirsty young prosecutor, spitting nails as her then-boss, the US Attorney for the Eastern District of New York—who had his eyes on higher office—shook Adam's hand and apologized for letting the case against him go as far as it had.

Playing magnanimous, Adam had nodded gravely, said all the right things about public servants simply doing their jobs, and with a wave for the news cameras, disappeared into his limousine.

Where he'd cracked a six-thousand-dollar bottle of Dom Perignon and made a solitary toast to a narrow escape from the law.

It had been his own damn fault that he'd come so close to being caught, because he *had* gotten cocky. He'd made a rare mistake, a minute one, but Madeline had used it like a crowbar to pry into his life until she'd damn near nailed him for stealing the *Lady in Red*.

The newly discovered Renoir masterpiece had been sold at Sotheby's to a Russian arms dealer, a glorified mobster who cynically expected a splashy show of good taste to purge the bloodstains from his billions. Adam couldn't stomach it, so he'd lifted the painting. Not for gain; he had his own billions. But because great art was sacred, and using it as a dishrag to wipe blood off the hands of a man who sold death was sacrilege.

Adam had simply saved the masterpiece from its unholy purpose.

It wasn't the first time, or the last, that he'd liberated great art from unclean hands. He told himself that it was his calling, but he couldn't deny that it was also a hell of a lot of fun. Outsmarting the best security systems money could buy taxed his brain in ways that managing his companies simply couldn't. Training for the physical demands kept him in Navy SEAL condition. And the adrenaline rush, well, that couldn't be duplicated. Not even by sex. No woman had ever thrilled him that intensely or challenged him so completely on every level.

But now the shoe was on the other foot. One of his own paintings—his favorite Monet—had been heisted clean off the wall of his Portofino villa.

Just the thought made his teeth grind.

Oh, he'd find it eventually; he had no doubt of that. He had the resources, both money and manpower. He was patient. He was relentless. And when he got his hands on the bastard who'd infiltrated his home—his sanctuary—he'd make him pay for his hubris.

But in the meantime, he had a more immediate concern. The insurance company, Hawthorne Mutual, was dragging its feet, balking at paying him the forty-four million dollars the Monet was insured for.

Forty-four million was a lot of money, even to a man like him. But it was the company's excuse for holding it up that really pissed him off. They needed to investigate the theft, they claimed, because Adam had once been a "person of interest" in the theft of the Renoir.

In short, Hawthorne's foot-dragging could be laid at Madeline's door. She'd damaged Adam's reputation, impugned his integrity. Cast a shadow of doubt over one of the richest men in the world.

Never mind that she'd been right about him.

Because she was visibly chomping at the bit, he moved as if he had all day, strolling to the far end of the room, where a leather sofa and club chairs clustered around a coordinating coffee table. This would be where clients chummied up with the partners after meetings, rubbing elbows over scotch and cigars while the lowly associates— like Madeline—scuttled back to their offices to do the actual work.

He poured himself an inch of scotch from the Waterford decanter on the table, then relaxed into the sofa, stretching one arm along the back, letting the other drape carelessly over the side, whiskey glass dangling from his fingers.

Her steel-gray eyes narrowed to slits. "What do you want, LeCroix? Why are you here?"

Lazily, he sipped his scotch, enjoying the angry flush that burned her cheeks. In the prosecutor's office, they'd called her the Pitbull. He was glad to see she'd lost none of her fire.

Watching her simmer, he remembered how her intensity had appealed to him. How much *she'd* appealed to him. Which was surprising, really. As a rule, he liked a solid armful of woman, and Madeline was barely there.

At the time, he'd told himself it was because she'd damn near taken him down. Naturally, he had to admire that.

But now he felt it again, that tug of attraction. Something about those suspicious eyes, that spring-loaded body, went straight to his groin. An image of her astride him, nails gouging his chest, eyes blazing with passion, flashed through his mind. Was she as hot-blooded in bed as she was in the courtroom?

Regrettably, he'd never find out. Because he was about to piss her off for life.

Dakota comes her into his bed and wants to keep her there for good, but all too soon the honeymoon over, and now Chris has to choose between losing her job of betraying Dakota . . . Will she sacrifice the career that de fines her to take a chance on love?

Are you hooked on Cara Connelly yet?
Don't miss the third book in the Save the Date *series,*

THE WEDDING BAND

coming from Avon Books in 2015!

CHRISTINA CASE IS the kind of Serious Reporter who still works in print and believes that news is meant to inform, not entertain. So how did her latest front-page story end up wrongly embarrassing a sitting senator? Her editor screwed up, that's how, and now Chris is out of a job unless she agrees to do the one thing she's sworn never to do—infiltrate a celebrity wedding.

Dakota Rain doesn't chase women; they chase him. As an A-list actor, a bona fide Movie Star, he's usually beating them off with a stick. He expected to do the same thing at his celebrity brother's wedding. So what's the deal with Crystie Case, the singer in the wedding band? Has he finally come up against a woman immune to his charms?

Chris goes along hoping for a story, but the weekend ends up being as enjoyable as it is revealing. The sweetly romantic newlyweds are open and friendly, and sexy

Dakota entices her into his bed and wants to keep her there for good. But all too soon the honeymoon's over, and now Chris has to choose between losing her job or betraying Dakota. Will she sacrifice the career that defines her to take a chance on love?

Give in to your impulses . . .
Read on for a sneak peek at four brand-new
e-book original tales of romance
from Avon Books.
Available now wherever e-books are sold.

RESCUED BY A STRANGER
By Lizbeth Selvig

CHASING MORGAN
BOOK FOUR: THE HUNTED SERIES
By Jennifer Ryan

THROWING HEAT
A DIAMONDS AND DUGOUTS NOVEL
By Jennifer Seasons

PRIVATE RESEARCH
AN EROTIC NOVELLA
By Sabrina Darby

An Excerpt from

RESCUED BY A STRANGER
by Lizbeth Selvig

When a stranger arrives in town on a vintage
motorcycle, Jill Carpenter has no idea her life
is about to change forever. She never expected
that her own personal knight in shining armor
would be an incredibly charming and handsome
southern man—but one with a deep secret. When
Jill's dreams of becoming an Olympic equestrian
start coming true, Chase's past finally returns to
haunt him. Can they get beyond dreams to find the
love that will rescue their two hearts? Find out in
the follow-up to *The Rancher and the Rock Star.*

"Angel?" Jill called. "C'mon, girl. Let's go get you something to eat." She'd responded to her new name all evening. Jill frowned.

Chase gave a soft, staccato, dog-calling whistle. Angel stuck her head out from a stall a third of the way down the aisle. "There she is. C'mon, girl."

Angel disappeared into the stall.

"Weird," Jill said, heading down the aisle.

At the door to a freshly bedded empty stall, they found Angel curled beside a mound of sweet, fragrant hay, staring up as if expecting them.

"Silly girl," Jill said. "You don't have to stay here. We're taking you home. Come."

Angel didn't budge. She rested her head between her paws and gazed through raised doggy brows. Chase led the way to the stall. "Everything all right, pup?" He stroked her head.

Jill reached for the dog, too, and her hand landed on Chase's. They both froze. Slowly he rotated his palm and wove his fingers through hers. The few minor fireworks she'd felt in the car earlier were nothing compared to the explosion now detonating up her arm and down her back.

"I've been trying to avoid this since I got off that dang horse." His voice cracked into a low whisper.

"Why?"

He stood and pulled her to her feet. "Because I am not a guy someone as young and good as you are should let do this."

"You've saved my life and rescued a dog. Are you trying to tell me I should be *worried* about you?"

She touched his face, bold enough in the dark to do what light had made her too shy to try.

"Maybe."

The hard, smooth fingertips of his free hand slid inexorably up her forearm and covered the hand on his cheek. Drawing it down to his side, he pulled her whole body close, and the little twister of excitement in her stomach burst into a thousand quicksilver thrills. Her eyelids slipped closed, and his next question touched them in warm puffs of breath.

"If I were to kiss you right now, would it be too soon?"

Her eyes flew open, and she searched his shadowy gaze, incredulous. "You're asking permission? Who does that?"

"Seemed like the right thing."

"Well, permission granted. Now hush."

She freed her hands, placed them on his cheeks, roughened with beard stubble, and rose on tiptoe to meet his mouth while he gripped the back of her head.

The soft kiss nearly knocked her breathless. Chase dropped more hot kisses on each corner of her mouth and down her chin, feathered her nose and her cheeks, and finally returned to her mouth. Again and again he plied her bottom lip with his teeth, stunning her with his insistent exploration. The pressure of his lips and the clean, masculine scent of his skin took away her equilibrium. She could only follow the motions of his head and revel in the heat stoking the fire in her belly.

He pulled away at last and pressed parted lips to her forehead.

An Excerpt from

CHASING MORGAN
Book Four: The Hunted Series
by Jennifer Ryan

Morgan Standish can see things other people
can't. She can see the past and future. These
hidden gifts have prevented her from getting
close to anyone—except FBI agent Tyler Reed.
Morgan is connected to him in a way even she can't
explain. She's solved several cases for him in the
past, but will her gifts be enough to bring down
a serial killer whose ultimate goal is to kill her?
Find out in Book Four of The Hunted Series.

Morgan's fingers flew across the laptop keyboard propped on her knees. She took a deep breath, cleared her mind, and looked out past her pink-painted toes resting on the railing and across her yard to the densely wooded area at the edge of her property. Her mind's eye found her guest winding his way through the trees. She still had time before Jack stepped out of the woods separating her land from his. She couldn't wait to meet him.

Images, knowings, they just came to her. She'd accepted that part of herself a long time ago. As she got older, she'd learned to use her gift to seek out answers.

She finished her buy-and-sell orders and switched from her day trading page to check her psychic website and read the questions submitted by customers. She answered several quickly, letting the others settle in her mind until the answers came to her.

One stood out. The innocuous question about getting a job held an eerie vibe.

The familiar strange pulsation came over her. The world disappeared, as though a door had slammed on reality. The images came to her like hammer blows, one right after the other, and she took the onslaught, knowing something important needed to be seen and understood.

An older woman lying in a bed, hooked up to a machine feeding her medication. Frail and ill, she had translucent skin and dark circles marring her tortured eyes. Her pain washed over Morgan like a tsunami.

The woman yelled at someone, her face contorted into something mean and hateful. An unhappy woman—one who'd spent her whole life blaming others and trying to make them as miserable as she was.

A pristine white pillow floating down, inciting panic, amplified to terror when it covered the woman's face, her frail body swallowed by the sheets.

Morgan had an overwhelming feeling of suffocation.

The woman tried desperately to suck in a breath, but couldn't. Unable to move her lethargic limbs, she lay petrified and helpless under his unyielding hands. Lights flashed on her closed eyelids.

Death came calling.

A man stood next to the bed, holding the pillow like a shield. His mouth opened on a contorted, evil, hysterical laugh that rang in her ears and made her skin crawl. She squeezed her eyes closed to blot out his malevolent image and thoughts.

Murderer!

The word rang in her head as the terrifying emotions overtook her.

Morgan threw up a wall in her mind, blocking the cascade of disturbing pictures and feelings. She took several deep breaths and concentrated on the white roses growing in profusion just below the porch railing. Their sweet fragrance filled the air. With every breath, she centered herself and found her inner calm, pushing out the anger and rage left over from the vision. Her body felt like a lead weight, lightening as her energy came back. The drowsiness faded with each new breath. She'd be fine in a few minutes.

The man on horseback emerged from the trees, coming toward her home. Her guest had arrived.

Focused on the computer screen, she slowly and meticulously typed her answer to the man who had asked about a job and inadvertently opened himself up to telling her who he really was at heart.

She replied simply:

You'll get the job, but you can't hide from what you did.
You need help. Turn yourself in to the police.

An Excerpt from

THROWING HEAT
A Diamonds and Dugouts Novel
by Jennifer Seasons

Nightclub manager Leslie Cutter has never
been one to back down from a bet. So when
Peter Kowalskin, pitcher for the Denver
Rush baseball team, bets her that she can't
keep her hands off of him, she's not about
to let the arrogant, gorgeous playboy win.
But as things heat up, this combustible pair
will have to decide just how much they're
willing to wager on one another . . . and on
a future that just might last forever.

"Is there something you want?" he demanded with a raised eyebrow, amused at being able to throw her words right back at her.

"You wish," Leslie retorted and tossed him a dismissive glance. Only he caught the gleam of interest in her eyes and knew her for the liar that she was.

Peter took a step toward her, closing the gap by a good foot until only an arm's reach separated them. He leaned forward and caged her in by placing a hand on each armrest of her chair. Her eyes widened the tiniest bit, but she held her ground.

"I wish many, many things."

"Really?" she questioned and shifted slightly away from him in her chair. "Such as what?"

Peter couldn't help noticing that her breathing had gone

shallow. How about that? "I wish to win the World Series this season." It would be a hell of a way to go out.

Her gaze landed on his mouth and flicked away. "Boring."

Humor sparked inside him at that, and he chuckled. "You want exciting?"

She shrugged. "Why not? Amuse me."

That worked for him. Hell yeah. If she didn't watch herself, he was going to excite the pants right off of her.

Just excitement, arousal, and sexual pleasure. That was what he was looking for this time around. And it was going to be fun leading her up to it.

But if he wanted her there, then he had to start.

Pushing until he'd tipped her chair back and only the balls of her feet were on the desk, her painted toes curling for a grip, Peter lowered his head until his mouth was against her ear. She smelled like coconut again, and his gut went tight.

"I wish I had you bent over this desk right here with your hot bare ass in the air."

She made a small sound in her throat and replied, "Less boring."

Peter grinned. Christ, the woman was tough. "Do you remember what I did to you that night in Miami? The thing that made you come hard, twice—one on top of the other?" He sure as hell did. It had involved his tongue, his fingers, and Leslie on all fours with her face buried in a pillow, moaning his name like she was begging for deliverance.

She tried to cover it, but he heard her quick intake of breath. "It wasn't that memorable."

Bullshit.

He slid a hand from the armrest and squeezed the top of her right leg, his thumb rubbing lazily back and forth on the skin of her inner thigh. Her muscles tensed, but she didn't pull away.

"Need a reminder?"

An Excerpt from

PRIVATE RESEARCH
An Erotic Novella
by Sabrina Darby

The last person Mina Cavallari expects to encounter in the depths of the National Archives while doing research on a thesis is Sebastian Graham, an outrageously sexy financial whiz. Sebastian is conducting a little research of his own into the history of what he thinks is just another London underworld myth, the fabled Harridan House. When he discovers that the private sex club still exists, he convinces Mina to join him on an odyssey into the intricacies of desire, pleasure, and, most surprisingly of all, love.

It was the most innocuous of sentences: "A cappuccino, please." Three words—without a verb to ground them, even. Yet, at the sound, my hand stilled mid-motion, my own paper coffee cup paused halfway between table and mouth. I looked over to the counter of the cafe. It was mid-afternoon, quieter than it had been when I'd come in earlier for a quick lunch, and only three people were in line behind the tall, slim-hipped, blond-haired man whose curve of shoulder and loose-limbed stance struck a chord in me as clearly as his voice.

Of course it couldn't be. In two years, surely, I had forgotten the exact tenor of his voice, was now confusing some other deep, posh English accent with his. Yet I watched the man, waited for him to turn around, as if there were any significant chance that in a city of eight million people, during the middle of the business day, I'd run into the one English acquaintance I had. At the National Archives, no less.

At the first glimpse of his profile, I sucked in my breath sharply, nearly dropping my coffee. Then he turned fully, looking around, likely for the counter with napkins and sugar. I watched his gaze pass over me and then snap back in recognition. I was both pleased and terrified. I'd come to London to put the past behind me, not to face down my demons. I'd been doing rather well these last months, but maybe this was part of some cosmic plan. As my time in England wound down, in order to move forward with my life, I had to come face to face with Sebastian Graham again.

"Mina!" He had an impressive way of making his voice heard across a room without shouting, and as he walked toward me, I put my cup down and stood, all too aware that while he looked like a fashionable professional about town, I still looked like a grad student——no makeup, hair pulled back in a ponytail, wearing jeans, sneakers, and a sweater.

"This is a pleasant surprise. Research for your dissertation? Anne Gracechurch, right?"

I nodded, bemused that he remembered a detail from what had surely been a throwaway conversation two years earlier. But of course I really shouldn't have been. Seb was brilliant, and brilliance wasn't the sort of thing that just faded away.

Neither, apparently, was his ability to make my pulse beat a bit faster or to tie up my tongue for a few seconds before I found my stride. He wasn't traditionally handsome, at least not in an American way. Too lean, too angular, hair receding a bit at the temples, and I was fairly certain he was now just shy of thirty. But I'd found him attractive from the first moment I'd met him.

I still did.

"That's right. What are you doing here? I mean, at the Archives."

"Ah." He shifted and smiled at me, and there was something about that smile that felt wicked and secretive. "A small genealogical project. Mind if I join you?"

I shook my head and sat back down. He pulled out his chair and sat, too, folding his long legs one over the other. Why was that sexy to me?

I focused on his face. He was pale. Much paler than he'd been in New Jersey, like he now spent most of his time indoors. Which should have been a turn-off. Yet, despite everything, I sat there imagining him in the kitchen of my apartment wearing nothing but boxer shorts. Apparently my memory was as good as his.

And I still remembered the crushing humiliation and disappointment of that last time we'd talked.